The Detectives

Agatha Christie is known throughout the world as the Queen of Crime. Her books have sold over a billion copies in English with another billion in foreign languages. She is the most widely published author of all time and in ay language, outsold only by the Bible and Shakespeare. She is the author of 80 crime novels and short story collections, 19 plays, and six novels written under the name of Mary Westmacott.

Agatha Christie's first novel, *The Mysterious Affair at Styles*, was written towards the end of the First World War, in which she served as a VAD. In it she created Hercule Poirot, the little Belgian detective who was destined to become the most popular detective in crime fiction since Sherlock Holmes. It was eventually published by The Bodley Head in 1920.

In 1926, after averaging a book a year, Agatha Christie wrote her masterpiece. *The Murder of Roger Ackroyd* was the first of her books to be published by Collins and marked the beginning of an author-publisher relationship which lasted for 50 years and well over 70 books. In 1943, for the first time, Agatha Christie adapted one of her own books for the stage: *And Then There Were None* proved to be a great success in the UK and USA. *The Mousetrap*, her most famous play of all, opened in 1952 and is the longest-running play in history.

Agatha Christie was made a Dame in 1971. She died in 1976, since when a number of books have been published posthumously: the bestselling novel *Sleeping Murder* appeared later that year, followed by her autobiography and the short story collections *Miss Marple's Final Cases, Problem at Pollensa Bay* and *While the Light Lasts*. In 1998 *Black Coffee* was the first of her plays to be n[   ]sborne.

Find [   ]**.com**

Have you got them all?

Poirot
- ❏ AC001 The ABC Murders
- ❏ AC002 After the Funeral
- ❏ AC003 Appointment With Death
- ❏ AC004 The Big Four
- ❏ AC005 Black Coffee *
- ❏ AC006 Cat Among the Pigeons
- ❏ AC007 The Clocks
- ❏ AC008 Curtain: Poirot's Last Case
- ❏ AC009 Death in the Clouds
- ❏ AC010 Death on the Nile
- ❏ AC011 Dumb Witness
- ❏ AC012 Evil Under the Sun
- ❏ AC013 Five Little Pigs
- ❏ AC014 Hercule Poirot's Christmas
- ❏ AC015 Hickory Dickory Dock
- ❏ AC016 The Hollow
- ❏ AC017 Lord Edgware Dies
- ❏ AC018 Murder in Mesopotamia
- ❏ AC019 The Murder of Roger Ackroyd
- ❏ AC020 The Murder on the Links
- ❏ AC021 Murder on the Orient Express
- ❏ AC022 The Mysterious Affair at Styles
- ❏ AC023 The Mystery of the Blue Train
- ❏ AC024 One, Two, Buckle My Shoe
- ❏ AC025 Peril at End House
- ❏ AC026 Sad Cypress
- ❏ AC027 Taken at the Flood
- ❏ AC028 Three Act Tragedy
- ❏ AC029 The Adventure of the Christmas Pudding
- ❏ AC030 The Labours of Hercules
- ❏ AC031 Murder in the Mews

* Novelisation by Charles Osborne

Special cost savings available when you call 01206 307999 to order
your books.
Save £££s now! Ring and have your credit card handy and quote
'ACSP' and the book's code from the list above. Please telephone
Mon-Fri 9.00am-5.00pm.

- ❏ AC032 Poirot Investigates
- ❏ AC033 Poirot's Early Cases

Poirot and Ariadne Oliver

- ❏ AC034 Cards on the Table
- ❏ AC035 Dead Man's Folly
- ❏ AC036 Elephants Can Remember
- ❏ AC037 Hallowe'en Party
- ❏ AC038 Mrs McGinty's Dead
- ❏ AC039 Third Girl

Ariadne Oliver

- ❏ AC040 The Pale Horse

Miss Marple

- ❏ AC041 At Bertram's Hotel
- ❏ AC042 The Body in the Library
- ❏ AC043 A Caribbean Mystery
- ❏ AC044 4.50 From Paddington
- ❏ AC045 The Mirror Crack'd from Side to Side
- ❏ AC046 The Moving Finger
- ❏ AC047 The Murder at the Vicarage
- ❏ AC048 A Murder is Announced
- ❏ AC049 Nemesis
- ❏ AC050 A Pocket Full of Rye
- ❏ AC051 Sleeping Murder
- ❏ AC052 They Do it with Mirrors
- ❏ AC053 Miss Marple's Final Cases
- ❏ AC054 The Thirteen Problems

Tommy & Tuppence

- ❏ AC055 By the Pricking of My Thumbs
- ❏ AC056 N or M?
- ❏ AC057 Postern of Fate
- ❏ AC058 The Secret Adversary
- ❏ AC059 Partners in Crime

Special cost savings available when you call 01206 307999 to order your books.
Save £££s now! Ring and have your credit card handy and quote 'ACSP' and the book's code from the list above. Please telephone Mon-Fri 9.00am-5.00pm.

Harley Quin

❑ AC060 The Mysterious Mr Quin

Parker Pyne

❑ AC061 Parker Pyne Investigates

Other Mysteries

❑ AC062 The Hound of Death
❑ AC063 The Listerdale Mystery
❑ AC064 Problem at Pollensa Bay
❑ AC065 While the Light Lasts
❑ AC066 And Then There Were None
❑ AC067 Crooked House
❑ AC068 Death Comes as the End
❑ AC069 Destination Unknown
❑ AC070 Endless Night
❑ AC071 The Man in the Brown Suit
❑ AC072 Ordeal By Innocence
❑ AC073 Passenger to Frankfurt
❑ AC074 The Sittaford Mystery
❑ AC075 Sparkling Cyanide
❑ AC076 Spider's Web *
❑ AC077 They Came to Baghdad
❑ AC078 The Unexpected Guest *
❑ AC079 Why Didn't They Ask Evans?
❑ AC080 Murder is Easy
❑ AC081 The Secret of Chimneys
❑ AC082 The Seven Dials Mystery
❑ AC083 Towards Zero

Memoirs

❑ AC084 An Autobiography

* *Novelisation by Charles Osborne*

Special cost savings available when you call 01206 307999 to order
your books.
Save £££s now! Ring and have your credit card handy and quote
'ACSP' and the book's code from the list above. Please telephone
Mon-Fri 9.00am-5.00pm.

Agatha Christie

THE DETECTIVES

Miss Marple, Poirot
and others

Short Stories

HarperCollins*Publishers*

**Explore the world of Agatha Christie at
www.agathachristie.com**

HarperCollins*Publishers*
77-85 Fulham Palace Road
Hammersmith, London W6 8JB
www.harpercollins.co.uk

This edition produced exclusively for Agatha Christie Limited
(a Chorion Company) 2005

The Man in the Mist © Agatha Christie Limited 1929
The Dead Harlequin © Agatha Christie Limited 1930
The Tuesday Night Club, The Thumbmark of St Peter and
The Affair at the Bungalow © Agatha Christie Limited 1932
The Gate of Baghdad and The Case of the Discontented Soldier
© Agatha Christie Limited 1934
How Does Your Garden Grow?, The Submarine Plans and
The Affair at the Victory Ball © Agatha Christie Limited 1974

ISBN 0 00 775219 9

Printed in Great Britain by
Clays Ltd, St Ives plc

Contents

75 YEARS OF MISS MARPLE

2005 marks the 75th anniversary of Agatha Christie's immortal spinster sleuth, Miss Marple.

All 14 Miss Marple books are available now at a special reduced price – ring 01026 307999 and quote 'ACSP' and the code from the lists at the front of this book.

Introducing The Queen of Crime

Agatha Christie's Creative Genius

Agatha Christie is recognised throughout the world as the Queen of Crime but where did she get her ideas from?

'Plots come to me at such odd moments, when I am walking along the street, or examining a hat shop . . . suddenly a splendid idea comes into my head.'

She made endless notes in dozens of notebooks, jotting down erratic ideas and potential plots and characters as they came to her:

'I usually have about half a dozen [notebooks] on hand and I used to make notes in them of ideas that struck me, or about some poison or drug, or a clever little bit of swindling that I had read about in the paper.'

Agatha Christie always said that there was no 'method' to her writing. She 'bashed out' the initial ideas herself on her old typewriter, or dictated her short stories onto a tape. She usually took no more than three months to write her novels. She felt that the real work was in working out all the plot details and clues in her head first, before writing the story down.

Her son-in-law Anthony Hicks once said:

'*You never saw her writing; [she never] shut herself away, like other writers do.*'

Influenced by the World Around Her

Agatha Christie wrote about the world she knew and saw, drawing on the military gents, lords and ladies, spinsters, widows and doctors of her family's circle of friends and acquaintances. She was a natural observer and her descriptions of village politics, local rivalries and family jealousies are often painfully accurate. Her grandson, Mathew Prichard, described her as a:

'*. . . person who listened more than she talked, who saw more than she was seen.*'

It was often the most everyday events and casual observations that triggered a new plot. Her second book, *The Secret Adversary*, stemmed from a conversation overheard in a tea shop:

"*Two people were talking at a table nearby, discussing somebody called Jane Fish. . . That, I thought, would make a good beginning to a story – a name overheard at a tea shop – an unusual name, so that whoever heard it remembered it. A name like Jane Fish, or perhaps Jane Finn would be even better.*'

Her next book, *The Murder on the Links*, was prompted by a newspaper article about a suspicious murder in France, and a theatre trip to see the actress Ruth Draper gave her the idea for another clever plot twist:

'*I thought how clever she was and how good her impersonations were. . . Thinking about her led me to the book* Lord Edgware Dies.'

Agatha's grandson also described how a trip to Wales and a local myth spawned another excellent murder mystery. His Granny Nora warned the family about a notoriously dangerous local stretch of road:

> ". . . the *gypsies cursed that corner years ago when old Harbour turned them off the land." Thus did [Agatha Christie] have the legend of Gypsy's Acre, on which the book* Endless Night *was based."*

Her notebooks make fascinating reading and the seeds for several stories are easily identified. In 1963, her notebook held details of a plot in development:

> *'West Indian book – Miss M? Poirot … B & E apparently devoted – actually B and G (Georgina) had affair for years . . . old 'frog' Major knows – has seen him before – he is killed.'*

A Caribbean Mystery was published in 1964 with the 'Old Frog' as the mystery's first victim. The Caribbean island is beautifully described and was probably based on St Lucia, an island that Agatha Christie had visited on holiday.

No prizes for guessing which title started as the notebook entry:

> *'Miss M, train coming from London to Reading? Man strangles a woman. The train was? 3.55, 3.19.'*

Of course we now know it was the *4:50 From Paddington*, but many of the hundreds of plots, counter plots and suspects from her fertile imagination never actually made it into print. As Agatha Christie said:

> *'Nothing turns out quite in the way that you thought it would when you are sketching out notes for the first chapter, or walking about muttering to yourself and seeing a story unroll.'*

The Detectives

Many of the notes that she jotted down were developed into short stories and published in illustrated weekly magazines like *The Sketch*. These were collected together later and published as books and sometimes the ideas were expanded into full length novels.

In this edition we've collected just ten of these masterpieces in miniature. Each of the stories features one of her favourite detectives and each is as satisfying and as complex as the best of her novels.

On the 75th anniversary of Miss Marple's debut, we are also able to offer you the chance to add to your collection with discounted editions of all her books – see the offer at the front of this book for details.

The Tuesday Night Club

'Unsolved mysteries.'

Raymond West blew out a cloud of smoke and repeated the words with a kind of deliberate self-conscious pleasure.

'Unsolved mysteries.'

He looked round him with satisfaction. The room was an old one with broad black beams across the ceiling and it was furnished with good old furniture that belonged to it. Hence Raymond West's approving glance. By profession he was a writer and he liked the atmosphere to be flawless. His Aunt Jane's house always pleased him as the right setting for her personality. He looked across the hearth to where she sat erect in the big grandfather chair. Miss Marple wore a black brocade dress, very much pinched in round the waist. Mechlin lace was arranged in a cascade down the front of the bodice. She had on black lace mittens, and a black lace cap surmounted the piled-up masses of her snowy hair. She was knitting – something white and soft and fleecy. Her faded blue eyes, benignant and kindly, surveyed her nephew and her nephew's guests with gentle pleasure. They rested first on Raymond himself, self-consciously debonair, then on Joyce Lemprière, the artist, with her close-cropped black head and queer hazel-green eyes, then on that well-groomed man of the world, Sir Henry Clithering. There were two other people in the room, Dr Pender, the elderly clergyman of the parish, and Mr Petherick, the solicitor, a dried-up little man with eyeglasses which he looked over and not through. Miss Marple gave a brief moment of attention to all these people and returned to her knitting with a gentle smile upon her lips.

Mr Petherick gave the dry little cough with which he usually prefaced his remarks.

'What is that you say, Raymond? Unsolved mysteries? Ha – and what about them?'

'Nothing about them,' said Joyce Lemprière. 'Raymond just likes the sound of the words and of himself saying them.'

Raymond West gave her a glance of reproach at which she threw back her head and laughed.

'He is a humbug, isn't he, Miss Marple?' she demanded. 'You know that, I am sure.'

Miss Marple smiled gently at him but made no reply.

'Life itself is an unsolved mystery,' said the clergyman gravely.

Raymond sat up in his chair and flung away his cigarette with an impulsive gesture.

'That's not what I mean. I was not talking philosophy,' he said. 'I was thinking of actual bare prosaic facts, things that have happened and that no one has ever explained.'

'I know just the sort of thing you mean, dear,' said Miss Marple. 'For instance Mrs Carruthers had a very strange experience yesterday morning. She bought two gills of peeled shrimps at Elliot's. She called at two other shops and when she got home she found she had not got the shrimps with her. She went back to the two shops she had visited but these shrimps had completely disappeared. Now that seems to me very remarkable.'

'A very fishy story,' said Sir Henry Clithering gravely.

'There are, of course, all kinds of possible explanations,' said Miss Marple, her cheeks growing slightly pinker with excitement. 'For instance, somebody else –'

'My dear Aunt,' said Raymond West with some amusement, 'I didn't mean that sort of village incident. I was thinking of murders and disappearances – the kind of thing that Sir Henry could tell us about by the hour if he liked.'

'But I never talk shop,' said Sir Henry modestly. 'No, I never talk shop.'

Sir Henry Clithering had been until lately Commissioner of Scotland Yard.

'I suppose there are a lot of murders and things that never are solved by the police,' said Joyce Lemprière.

'That is an admitted fact, I believe,' said Mr Petherick.

'I wonder,' said Raymond West, 'what class of brain really succeeds best in unravelling a mystery? One always feels that the average police detective must be hampered by lack of imagination.'

'That is the layman's point of view,' said Sir Henry dryly.

'You really want a committee,' said Joyce, smiling. 'For psychology and imagination go to the writer –'

She made an ironical bow to Raymond but he remained serious.

'The art of writing gives one an insight into human nature,' he said gravely. 'One sees, perhaps, motives that the ordinary person would pass by.'

'I know, dear,' said Miss Marple, 'that your books are very clever. But do you think that people are really so unpleasant as you make them out to be?'

'My dear Aunt,' said Raymond gently, 'keep your beliefs. Heaven forbid that *I* should in any way shatter them.'

'I mean,' said Miss Marple, puckering her brow a little as she counted the stitches in her knitting, 'that so many people seem to me not to be either bad or good, but simply, you know, very silly.'

Mr Petherick gave his dry little cough again.

'Don't you think, Raymond,' he said, 'that you attach too much weight to imagination? Imagination is a very dangerous thing, as we lawyers know only too well. To be able to sift evidence impartially, to take the facts and look at them as facts – that seems to me the only logical method of arriving at the truth. I may add that in my experience it is the only one that succeeds.'

'Bah!' cried Joyce, flinging back her black head indignantly. 'I bet I could beat you all at this game. I am not only a woman – and say what you like, women have an intuition that is denied to men – I am an artist as well. I see things that you don't. And then, too, as an artist I have knocked about among all sorts and conditions of people. I know life as darling Miss Marple here cannot possibly know it.'

'I don't know about that, dear,' said Miss Marple. 'Very painful and distressing things happen in villages sometimes.'

'May I speak?' said Dr Pender smiling. 'It is the fashion nowadays to decry the clergy, I know, but we hear things, we know a side of human character which is a sealed book to the outside world.'

'Well,' said Joyce, 'it seems to me we are a pretty representative gathering. How would it be if we formed a Club? What is today? Tuesday? We will call it The Tuesday Night Club. It is to meet every week, and each member in turn has to propound a problem. Some mystery of which they have personal knowledge, and to which, of course, they know the answer. Let me see, how many are we? One, two, three, four, five. We ought really to be six.'

'You have forgotten me, dear,' said Miss Marple, smiling brightly.

Joyce was slightly taken aback, but she concealed the fact quickly.

'That would be lovely, Miss Marple,' she said. 'I didn't think you would care to play.'

'I think it would be very interesting,' said Miss Marple, 'especially with so many clever gentlemen present. I am afraid I am not very clever myself, but living all these years in St Mary Mead does give one an insight into human nature.'

'I am sure your co-operation will be very valuable,' said Sir Henry, courteously.

'Who is going to start?' said Joyce.

'I think there is no doubt as to that,' said Dr Pender, 'when we have the great good fortune to have such a distinguished man as Sir Henry staying with us –'

He left his sentence unfinished, making a courtly bow in the direction of Sir Henry.

The latter was silent for a minute or two. At last he sighed and recrossed his legs and began:

'It is a little difficult for me to select just the kind of thing you want, but I think, as it happens, I know of an instance which fits these conditions very aptly. You may have seen some mention of the case in the papers of a year ago. It was laid aside at the time as an unsolved mystery, but, as it happens, the solution came into my hands not very many days ago.

'The facts are very simple. Three people sat down to a supper consisting, amongst other things, of tinned lobster. Later in the night, all three were taken ill, and a doctor was hastily summoned. Two of the people recovered, the third one died.'

'Ah!' said Raymond approvingly.

'As I say, the facts as such were very simple. Death was considered to be due to ptomaine poisoning, a certificate was given to that effect, and the victim was duly buried. But things did not rest at that.'

Miss Marple nodded her head.

'There was talk, I suppose,' she said, 'there usually is.'

'And now I must describe the actors in this little drama. I will call the husband and wife Mr and Mrs Jones, and the wife's companion Miss Clark. Mr Jones was a traveller for a firm of manufacturing chemists. He was a good-looking man in a kind of coarse, florid way, aged about fifty. His wife was a rather commonplace woman, of about forty-five. The companion, Miss Clark, was a woman of sixty, a stout cheery woman with a beaming rubicund face. None of them, you might say, very interesting.

'Now the beginning of the troubles arose in a very curious way. Mr Jones had been staying the previous night at a small commercial hotel in Birmingham. It happened that the blotting paper in the blotting book had been put in fresh that day, and the chambermaid, having apparently nothing better to do, amused herself by studying the blotter in the mirror just after Mr Jones had been writing a letter there. A few days later there was a report in the papers of the death of Mrs Jones as the result of eating tinned lobster, and the chambermaid then imparted to her fellow servants the words that she had deciphered on the blotting pad. They were as follows: *Entirely dependent on my wife . . . when she is dead I will . . . hundreds and thousands . . .*

'You may remember that there had recently been a case of a wife being poisoned by her husband. It needed very little to fire the imagination of these maids. Mr Jones had planned to do away with his wife and inherit hundreds of thousands of pounds! As it happened one of the maids had relations living in the small market town where the Joneses resided. She wrote to them, and they in return wrote to her. Mr Jones, it seemed, had been very attentive to the local doctor's daughter, a good-looking young woman of thirty-three. Scandal began to hum. The Home Secretary was petitioned. Numerous anonymous letters poured into Scotland Yard all accusing Mr Jones of having murdered his wife. Now I may say that not for one moment did we think there was anything in it except idle village talk and gossip. Nevertheless, to quiet public opinion an exhumation order was granted. It was one of these cases of popular superstition based on nothing solid whatever, which proved to be so surprisingly justified. As a result of the autopsy sufficient arsenic was found to make it quite clear that the deceased lady had died of arsenical poisoning. It was for

Scotland Yard working with the local authorities to prove how that arsenic had been administered, and by whom.'

'Ah!' said Joyce. 'I like this. This is the real stuff.'

'Suspicion naturally fell on the husband. He benefited by his wife's death. Not to the extent of the hundreds of thousands romantically imagined by the hotel chambermaid, but to the very solid amount of £8000. He had no money of his own apart from what he earned, and he was a man of somewhat extravagant habits with a partiality for the society of women. We investigated as delicately as possible the rumour of his attachment to the doctor's daughter; but while it seemed clear that there had been a strong friendship between them at one time, there had been a most abrupt break two months previously, and they did not appear to have seen each other since. The doctor himself, an elderly man of a straightforward and unsuspicious type, was dumbfounded at the result of the autopsy. He had been called in about midnight to find all three people suffering. He had realized immediately the serious condition of Mrs Jones, and had sent back to his dispensary for some opium pills, to allay the pain. In spite of all his efforts, however, she succumbed, but not for a moment did he suspect that anything was amiss. He was convinced that her death was due to a form of botulism. Supper that night had consisted of tinned lobster and salad, trifle and bread and cheese. Unfortunately none of the lobster remained – it had all been eaten and the tin thrown away. He had interrogated the young maid, Gladys Linch. She was terribly upset, very tearful and agitated, and he found it hard to get her to keep to the point, but she declared again and again that the tin had not been distended in any way and that the lobster had appeared to her in a perfectly good condition.

'Such were the facts we had to go upon. If Jones had feloniously administered arsenic to his wife, it seemed clear that it could not have been done in any of the things eaten at supper, as all three persons had partaken of the meal. Also – another point – Jones himself had returned from Birmingham just as supper was being brought in to table, so that he would have had no opportunity of doctoring any of the food beforehand.'

'What about the companion?' asked Joyce – 'the stout woman with the good-humoured face.'

Sir Henry nodded.

'We did not neglect Miss Clark, I can assure you. But it seemed doubtful what motive she could have had for the crime. Mrs Jones left her no legacy of any kind and the net result of her employer's death was that she had to seek for another situation.'

'That seems to leave her out of it,' said Joyce thoughtfully.

'Now one of my inspectors soon discovered a significant fact,' went on Sir Henry. 'After supper on that evening Mr Jones had gone down to the kitchen and had demanded a bowl of cornflour for his wife who had complained of not feeling well. He had waited in the kitchen until Gladys Linch prepared it, and then carried it up to his wife's room himself. That, I admit, seemed to clinch the case.'

The lawyer nodded.

'Motive,' he said, ticking the points off on his fingers. 'Opportunity. As a traveller for a firm of druggists, easy access to the poison.'

'And a man of weak moral fibre,' said the clergyman.

Raymond West was staring at Sir Henry.

'There is a catch in this somewhere,' he said. 'Why did you not arrest him?'

Sir Henry smiled rather wryly.

'That is the unfortunate part of the case. So far all had gone swimmingly, but now we come to the snags. Jones was not arrested because on interrogating Miss Clark she told us that the whole of the bowl of cornflour was drunk not by Mrs Jones but by her.

'Yes, it seems that she went to Mrs Jones's room as was her

custom. Mrs Jones was sitting up in bed and the bowl of cornflour was beside her.

'"I am not feeling a bit well, Milly," she said. "Serves me right, I suppose, for touching lobster at night. I asked Albert to get me a bowl of cornflour, but now that I have got it I don't seem to fancy it."

'"A pity," commented Miss Clark – "it is nicely made too, no lumps. Gladys is really quite a nice cook. Very few girls nowadays seem to be able to make a bowl of cornflour nicely. I declare I quite fancy it myself, I am that hungry."

'"I should think you were with your foolish ways," said Mrs Jones.

'I must explain,' broke off Sir Henry, 'that Miss Clark, alarmed at her increasing stoutness, was trying to slim and was doing a course of what is popularly known as "banting".'

'"It is not good for you, Milly, it really isn't," urged Mrs Jones. "If the Lord made you stout he meant you to be stout. You drink up that bowl of cornflour. It will do you all the good in the world."

'And straight away Miss Clark set to and did in actual fact finish the bowl. So, you see, that knocked our case against the husband to pieces. Asked for an explanation of the words on the blotting book Jones gave one readily enough. The letter, he explained, was in answer to one written from his brother in Australia who had applied to him for money. He had written, pointing out that he was entirely dependent on his wife. When his wife was dead he would have control of money and would assist his brother if possible. He regretted his inability to help but pointed out that there were hundreds and thousands of people in the world in the same unfortunate plight.'

'And so the case fell to pieces?' said Dr Pender.

'And so the case fell to pieces,' said Sir Henry gravely. 'We could not take the risk of arresting Jones with nothing to go upon.'

There was silence and then Joyce said, 'And that is all, is it?'

'That is the case as it has stood for the last year. The true solution is now in the hands of Scotland Yard, and in two or three days' time you will probably read of it in the newspapers.'

'The true solution,' said Joyce thoughtfully. 'I wonder. Let's all think for five minutes and then speak.'

Raymond West nodded and noted the time on his watch. When the five minutes were up he looked over at Dr Pender.

'Will you speak first?' he said.

The old man shook his head. 'I confess,' he said, 'that I am utterly baffled. I can but think that the husband in some way must be the guilty party, but how he did it I cannot imagine. I can only suggest that he must have given her the poison in some way that has not yet been discovered, although how in that case it should have come to light after all this time I cannot imagine.'

'Joyce?'

'The companion!' said Joyce decidedly. 'The companion every time! How do we know what motive she may have had? Just because she was old and stout and ugly it doesn't follow that she wasn't in love with Jones herself. She may have hated the wife for some other reason. Think of being a companion – always having to be pleasant and agree and stifle yourself and bottle yourself up. One day she couldn't bear it any longer and then she killed her. She probably put the arsenic in the bowl of cornflour and all that story about eating it herself is a lie.'

'Mr Petherick?'

The lawyer joined the tips of his fingers together professionally. 'I should hardly like to say. On the facts I should hardly like to say.'

'But you have got to, Mr Petherick,' said Joyce. 'You can't reserve judgement and say "without prejudice", and be legal. You have got to play the game.'

'On the facts,' said Mr Petherick, 'there seems nothing to be said. It is my private opinion, having seen, alas, too many cases of this kind, that the husband was guilty. The only explanation that will cover the facts seems to be that Miss Clark for some reason or other deliberately sheltered him. There may have been some financial arrangement made between them. He might realize that he would be suspected, and she, seeing only a future of poverty before her, may have agreed to tell the story of drinking the cornflour in return for a substantial sum to be paid to her privately. If that was the case it was of course most irregular. Most irregular indeed.'

'I disagree with you all,' said Raymond. 'You have forgotten the one important factor in the case. *The doctor's daughter.* I will give you my reading of the case. The tinned lobster was bad. It accounted for the poisoning symptoms. The doctor was sent for. He finds Mrs Jones, who has eaten more lobster than the others, in great pain, and he sends, as you told us, for some opium pills. He does not go himself, he sends. Who will give the messenger the opium pills? Clearly his daughter. Very likely she dispenses his medicines for him. She is in love with Jones and at this moment all the worst instincts in her nature rise and she realizes that the means to procure his freedom are in her hands. The pills she sends contain pure white arsenic. That is my solution.'

'And now, Sir Henry, tell us,' said Joyce eagerly.

'One moment,' said Sir Henry. 'Miss Marple has not yet spoken.'

Miss Marple was shaking her head sadly.

'Dear, dear,' she said. 'I have dropped another stitch. I have been so interested in the story. A sad case, a very sad case. It reminds me of old Mr Hargraves who lived up at the Mount. His wife never had the least suspicion – until he died, leaving all his money to a woman he had been living with and by whom he had five children. She had at one time been their housemaid. Such a nice girl, Mrs Hargraves always said – thoroughly to be relied upon to turn the mattresses every day

11

– except Fridays, of course. And there was old Hargraves keeping this woman in a house in the neighbouring town and continuing to be a Churchwarden and to hand round the plate every Sunday.'

'My dear Aunt Jane,' said Raymond with some impatience. 'What has dead and gone Hargraves got to do with the case?'

'This story made me think of him at once,' said Miss Marple. 'The facts are so very alike, aren't they? I suppose the poor girl has confessed now and that is how you know, Sir Henry.'

'What girl?' said Raymond. 'My dear Aunt, what *are* you talking about?'

'That poor girl, Gladys Linch, of course – the one who was so terribly agitated when the doctor spoke to her – and well she might be, poor thing. I hope that wicked Jones is hanged, I am sure, making that poor girl a murderess. I suppose they will hang her too, poor thing.'

'I think, Miss Marple, that you are under a slight misapprehension,' began Mr Petherick.

But Miss Marple shook her head obstinately and looked across at Sir Henry.

'I am right, am I not? It seems so clear to me. The hundreds and thousands – and the trifle – I mean, one cannot miss it.'

'What about the trifle and the hundreds and thousands?' cried Raymond.

His aunt turned to him.

'Cooks nearly always put hundreds and thousands on trifle, dear,' she said. 'Those little pink and white sugar things. Of course when I heard that they had trifle for supper and that the husband had been writing to someone about hundreds and thousands, I naturally connected the two things together. That is where the arsenic was – in the hundreds and thousands. He left it with the girl and told her to put it on the trifle.'

'But that is impossible,' said Joyce quickly. 'They all ate the trifle.'

'Oh, no,' said Miss Marple. 'The companion was banting, you remember. You never eat anything like trifle if you are banting; and I expect Jones just scraped the hundreds and thousands off his share and left them at the side of his plate. It was a clever idea, but a very wicked one.'

The eyes of the others were all fixed upon Sir Henry.

'It is a very curious thing,' he said slowly, 'but Miss Marple happens to have hit upon the truth. Jones had got Gladys Linch into trouble, as the saying goes. She was nearly desperate. He wanted his wife out of the way and promised to marry Gladys when his wife was dead. He doctored the hundreds and thousands and gave them to her with instructions how to use them. Gladys Linch died a week ago. Her child died at birth and Jones had deserted her for another woman. When she was dying she confessed the truth.'

There was a few moments' silence and then Raymond said:

'Well, Aunt Jane, this is one up to you. I can't think how on earth you managed to hit upon the truth. I should never have thought of the little maid in the kitchen being connected with the case.'

'No, dear,' said Miss Marple, 'but you don't know as much of life as I do. A man of that Jones type – coarse and jovial. As soon as I heard there was a pretty young girl in the house I felt sure that he would not have left her alone. It is all very distressing and painful, and not a very nice thing to talk about. I can't tell you the shock it was to Mrs Hargraves, and a nine days' wonder in the village.'

The Thumb Mark of St Peter

'And now, Aunt Jane, it is up to you,' said Raymond West.

'Yes, Aunt Jane, we are expecting something really spicy,' chimed in Joyce Lemprière.

'Now, you are laughing at me, my dears,' said Miss Marple placidly. 'You think that because I have lived in this out-of-the-way spot all my life I am not likely to have had any very interesting experiences.'

'God forbid that I should ever regard village life as peaceful and uneventful,' said Raymond with fervour. 'Not after the horrible revelations we have heard from you! The cosmopolitan world seems a mild and peaceful place compared with St Mary Mead.'

'Well, my dear,' said Miss Marple, 'human nature is much the same everywhere, and, of course, one has opportunities of observing it at close quarters in a village.'

'You really are unique, Aunt Jane,' cried Joyce. 'I hope you don't mind me calling you Aunt Jane?' she added. 'I don't know why I do it.'

'Don't you, my dear?' said Miss Marple.

She looked up for a moment or two with something quizzical in her glance, which made the blood flame to the girl's cheeks. Raymond West fidgeted and cleared his throat in a somewhat embarrassed manner.

Miss Marple looked at them both and smiled again, and bent her attention once more to her knitting.

'It is true, of course, that I have lived what is called a very uneventful life, but I have had a lot of experience in solving different little problems that have arisen. Some of them have been really quite ingenious, but it would be no good telling them to you, because they are about such unimportant things that you would not be interested – just things like: Who cut the meshes of Mrs Jones's string bag? and why Mrs Sims only wore her new fur coat once. Very interesting things, really, to any student of human nature. No, the only experience I can remember that would be of interest to you is the one about my poor niece Mabel's husband.

'It is about ten or fifteen years ago now, and happily it is all over and done with, and everyone has forgotten about it. People's memories are very short – a lucky thing, I always think.'

Miss Marple paused and murmured to herself:

'I must just count this row. The decreasing is a little awkward. One, two, three, four, five, and then three purl; that is right. Now, what was I saying? Oh, yes, about poor Mabel.

'Mabel was my niece. A nice girl, really a very nice girl, but just a trifle what one might call *silly*. Rather fond of being melodramatic and of saying a great deal more than she meant whenever she was upset. She married a Mr Denman when she was twenty-two, and I am afraid it was not a very happy marriage. I had hoped very much that the attachment would not come to anything, for Mr Denman was a man of very violent temper – not the kind of man who would be patient with Mabel's foibles – and I also learned that there was insanity in his family. However, girls were just as obstinate then as they are now, and as they always will be. And Mabel married him.

'I didn't see very much of her after her marriage. She came to stay with me once or twice, and they asked me there several times, but, as a matter of fact, I am not very fond of staying in other people's houses, and I always managed to make some excuse. They had been married ten years when Mr Denman died suddenly. There were no children, and he left all his money to Mabel. I wrote, of course, and offered to come to Mabel if she wanted me; but she wrote back a very sensible letter, and I gathered that she was not altogether overwhelmed by grief. I thought that was only natural, because I knew they had not been getting on together for some time. It was not until about three months afterwards that I got a most hysterical letter from Mabel, begging me to come to her, and saying that things were going from bad to worse, and she couldn't stand it much longer.

'So, of course,' continued Miss Marple, 'I put Clara on board wages and sent the plate and the King Charles tankard to the bank, and I went off at once. I found Mabel in a very nervous state. The house, Myrtle Dene, was a fairly large one, very comfortably furnished. There was a cook and a house-parlourmaid as well as a nurse-attendant to look after old Mr Denman, Mabel's husband's father, who was what is called "not quite right in the head". Quite peaceful and well behaved, but distinctly odd at times. As I say, there was insanity in the family.

'I was really shocked to see the change in Mabel. She was a mass of nerves, twitching all over, yet I had the greatest difficulty in making her tell me what the trouble was. I got at it, as one always does get at these things, indirectly. I asked her about some friends of hers she was always mentioning in her letters, the Gallaghers. She said, to my surprise, that she hardly ever saw them nowadays. Other friends whom I mentioned elicited the same remark. I spoke to her then of the folly of shutting herself up and brooding, and especially of the silliness of cutting herself adrift from her friends. Then she came bursting out with the truth.

'"It is not my doing, it is theirs. There is not a soul in the place who will speak to me now. When I go down the High

16

Street they all get out of the way so that they shan't have to meet me or speak to me. I am like a kind of leper. It is awful, and I can't bear it any longer. I shall have to sell the house and go abroad. Yet why should I be driven away from a home like this? I have done nothing."

'I was more disturbed than I can tell you. I was knitting a comforter for old Mrs Hay at the time, and in my perturbation I dropped two stitches and never discovered it until long after.

'"My dear Mabel," I said, "you amaze me. But what is the cause of all this?"

'Even as a child Mabel was always difficult. I had the greatest difficulty in getting her to give me a straightforward answer to my question. She would only say vague things about wicked talk and idle people who had nothing better to do than gossip, and people who put ideas into other people's heads.

'"That is all quite clear to me," I said. "There is evidently some story being circulated about you. But what that story is you must know as well as anyone. And you are going to tell me."

'"It is so wicked," moaned Mabel.

'"Of course it is wicked," I said briskly. "There is nothing that you can tell me about people's minds that would astonish or surprise me. Now, Mabel, will you tell me in plain English what people are saying about you?"

'Then it all came out.

'It seemed that Geoffrey Denman's death, being quite sudden and unexpected, gave rise to various rumours. In fact – and in plain English as I had put it to her – people were saying that she had poisoned her husband.

'Now, as I expect you know, there is nothing more cruel than talk, and there is nothing more difficult to combat. When people say things behind your back there is nothing you can refute or deny, and the rumours go on growing and growing, and no one can stop them. I was quite certain of one thing:

Mabel was quite incapable of poisoning anyone. And I didn't see why life should be ruined for her and her home made unbearable just because in all probability she had been doing something silly and foolish.

'"There is no smoke without fire," I said. "Now, Mabel, you have got to tell me what started people off on this tack. There must have been something."

'Mabel was very incoherent, and declared there was nothing – nothing at all, except, of course, that Geoffrey's death had been very sudden. He had seemed quite well at supper that evening, and had taken violently ill in the night. The doctor had been sent for, but the poor man had died a few minutes after the doctor's arrival. Death had been thought to be the result of eating poisoned mushrooms.

'"Well," I said, "I suppose a sudden death of that kind might start tongues wagging, but surely not without some additional facts. Did you have a quarrel with Geoffrey or anything of that kind?"

'She admitted that she had had a quarrel with him on the preceding morning at breakfast time.

'"And the servants heard it, I suppose?" I asked.

'"They weren't in the room."

'"No, my dear," I said, "but they probably were fairly near the door outside."

'I knew the carrying power of Mabel's high-pitched hysterical voice only too well. Geoffrey Denman, too, was a man given to raising his voice loudly when angry.

'"What did you quarrel about?" I asked.

'"Oh, the usual things. It was always the same things over and over again. Some little thing would start us off, and then Geoffrey became impossible and said abominable things, and I told him what I thought of him."

'"There had been a lot of quarrelling, then?" I asked.

'"It wasn't my fault –"

18

'"My dear child," I said, "it doesn't matter whose fault it was. That is not what we are discussing. In a place like this everybody's private affairs are more or less public property. You and your husband were always quarrelling. You had a particularly bad quarrel one morning, and that night your husband died suddenly and mysteriously. Is that all, or is there anything else?"

'"I don't know what you mean by anything else," said Mabel sullenly.

'"Just what I say, my dear. If you have done anything silly, don't for Heaven's sake keep it back now. I only want to do what I can to help you."

'"Nothing and nobody can help me," said Mabel wildly, "except death."

'"Have a little more faith in Providence, dear," I said. "Now then, Mabel, I know perfectly well there *is* something else that you are keeping back."

'I always did know, even when she was a child, when she was not telling me the whole truth. It took a long time, but I got it out at last. She had gone down to the chemist's that morning and had bought some arsenic. She had had, of course, to sign the book for it. Naturally, the chemist had talked.

'"Who is your doctor?" I asked.

'"Dr Rawlinson."

'I knew him by sight. Mabel had pointed him out to me the other day. To put it in perfectly plain language he was what I would describe as an old dodderer. I have had too much experience of life to believe in the infallibility of doctors. Some of them are clever men and some of them are not, and half the time the best of them don't know what is the matter with you. I have no truck with doctors and their medicines myself.

'I thought things over, and then I put my bonnet on and went to call on Dr Rawlinson. He was just what I had thought him – a nice old man, kindly, vague, and so short-sighted as to be pitiful, slightly deaf, and, withal, touchy and sensitive to the last degree. He was on his high horse at once when I mentioned Geoffrey Denman's death, talked for a long time about various kinds of fungi, edible and otherwise. He had questioned the cook, and she had admitted that one or two of the mushrooms cooked had been "a little queer", but as the shop had sent them she thought they must be all right. The more she had thought about them since, the more she was convinced that their appearance was unusual.

'"She would be," I said. "They would start by being quite like mushrooms in appearance, and they would end by being orange with purple spots. There is nothing that class cannot remember if it tries."

'I gathered that Denman had been past speech when the doctor got to him. He was incapable of swallowing, and had died within a few minutes. The doctor seemed perfectly satisfied with the certificate he had given. But how much of that was obstinacy and how much of it was genuine belief I could not be sure.

'I went straight home and asked Mabel quite frankly why she had bought arsenic.

'"You must have had some idea in your mind," I pointed out.

'Mabel burst into tears. "I wanted to make away with myself," she moaned. "I was too unhappy. I thought I would end it all."

'"Have you the arsenic still?" I asked.

'"No, I threw it away."

'I sat there turning things over and over in my mind.

'"What happened when he was taken ill? Did he call you?"

'"No." She shook her head. "He rang the bell violently. He must have rung several times. At last Dorothy, the house-parlourmaid, heard it, and she waked the cook up, and they came down. When Dorothy saw him she was frightened. He was rambling and delirious. She left the cook with him and came rushing to me. I got up and went to him. Of course I saw at once he was dreadfully ill. Unfortunately Brewster, who looks after old Mr Denman, was away for the night, so there was no one who knew what to do. I sent Dorothy off for the doctor, and cook and I stayed with him, but after a few minutes I couldn't bear it any longer; it was too dreadful. I ran away back to my room and locked the door."

' "Very selfish and unkind of you," I said; "and no doubt that conduct of yours has done nothing to help you since, you may be sure of that. Cook will have repeated it everywhere. Well, well, this is a bad business."

'Next I spoke to the servants. The cook wanted to tell me about the mushrooms, but I stopped her. I was tired of these mushrooms. Instead, I questioned both of them very closely about their master's condition on that night. They both agreed that he seemed to be in great agony, that he was unable to swallow, and he could only speak in a strangled voice, and when he did speak it was only rambling – nothing sensible.

' "What did he say when he was rambling?" I asked curiously.

' "Something about some fish, wasn't it?" turning to the other.

'Dorothy agreed.

' "A heap of fish," she said; "some nonsense like that. I could see at once he wasn't in his right mind, poor gentleman."

'There didn't seem to be any sense to be made out of that. As a last resource I went up to see Brewster, who was a gaunt, middle-aged woman of about fifty.

' "It is a pity that I wasn't here that night," she said. "Nobody seems to have tried to do anything for him until the doctor came."

' "I suppose he was delirious," I said doubtfully; "but that is not a symptom of ptomaine poisoning, is it?"

' "It depends," said Brewster.

'I asked her how her patient was getting on.

'She shook her head.

'"He is pretty bad," she said.

'"Weak?"

'"Oh no, he is strong enough physically – all but his eye-sight. That is failing badly. He may outlive all of us, but his mind is failing very fast now. I have already told both Mr and Mrs Denman that he ought to be in an institution, but Mrs Denman wouldn't hear of it at any price."

'I will say for Mabel that she always had a kindly heart.

'Well, there the thing was. I thought it over in every aspect, and at last I decided that there was only one thing to be done. In view of the rumours that were going about, permission must be applied for to exhume the body, and a proper post-mortem must be made and lying tongues quietened once and for all. Mabel, of course, made a fuss, mostly on sentimental grounds – disturbing the dead man in his peaceful grave, etc., etc. – but I was firm.

'I won't make a long story of this part of it. We got the order and they did the autopsy, or whatever they call it, but the result was not so satisfactory as it might have been. There was no trace of arsenic – that was all to the good – but the actual words of the report were *that there was nothing to show by what means deceased had come to his death.*

'So, you see, that didn't lead us out of trouble altogether. People went on talking – about rare poisons impossible to detect, and rubbish of that sort. I had seen the pathologist who had done the post-mortem, and I had asked him several questions, though he tried his best to get out of answering most of them; but I got out of him that he considered it highly unlikely that the poisoned mushrooms were the cause of death. An idea was simmering in my mind, and I asked him what poison, if any, could have been employed to obtain that result. He made a long explanation to me, most of which, I must admit, I did not follow, but it amounted to this: That death might have been due to some strong vegetable alkaloid.

'The idea I had was this: Supposing the taint of insanity was in Geoffrey Denman's blood also, might he not have made away with himself? He had, at one period of his life, studied medicine, and he would have a good knowledge of poisons and their effects.

'I didn't think it sounded very likely, but it was the only thing I could think of. And I was nearly at my wits' end, I can tell you. Now, I dare say you modern young people will laugh, but when I am in really bad trouble I always say a little prayer to myself – anywhere, when I am walking along the street, or at a bazaar. And I always get an answer. It may be some trifling thing, apparently quite unconnected with the subject, but there it is. I had that text pinned over my bed when I was a little girl: *Ask and you shall receive*. On the morning that I am telling you about, I was walking along the High Street, and I was praying hard. I shut my eyes, and when I opened them, what do you think was the first thing that I saw?'

Five faces with varying degrees of interest were turned to Miss Marple. It may be safely assumed, however, that no one would have guessed the answer to the question right.

'I saw,' said Miss Marple impressively, '*the window of the fishmonger's shop*. There was only one thing in it, *a fresh haddock*.'

She looked round triumphantly.

'Oh, my God!' said Raymond West. 'An answer to prayer – a fresh haddock!'

'Yes, Raymond,' said Miss Marple severely, 'and there is no need to be profane about it. The hand of God is everywhere. The first thing I saw were the black spots – the marks of St Peter's thumb. That is the legend, you know. St Peter's thumb. And that brought things home to me. I needed faith, the ever true faith of St Peter. I connected the two things together, faith – and fish.'

Sir Henry blew his nose rather hurriedly. Joyce bit her lip.

'Now what did that bring to my mind? Of course, both the cook and house-parlourmaid mentioned fish as being one of the things spoken of by the dying man. I was convinced, absolutely convinced, that there was some solution of the mystery to be found in these words. I went home determined to get to the bottom of the matter.'

She paused.

'Has it ever occurred to you,' the old lady went on, 'how much we go by what is called, I believe, the context? There is a place on Dartmoor called Grey Wethers. If you were talking to a farmer there and mentioned Grey Wethers, he would probably conclude that you were speaking of these stone circles, yet it is possible that you might be speaking of the atmosphere; and in the same way, if you were meaning the stone circles, an outsider, hearing a fragment of the conversation, might think you meant the weather. So when we repeat a conversation, we don't, as a rule, repeat the actual words; we put in some other words that seem to us to mean exactly the same thing.

'I saw both the cook and Dorothy separately. I asked the cook if she was quite sure that her master had really mentioned a heap of fish. She said she was quite sure.

'"Were these his exact words," I asked, "or did he mention some particular kind of fish?"

'"That's it," said the cook; "it was some particular kind of fish, but I can't remember what now. A heap of – now what was it? Not any of the fish you send to table. Would it be a perch now – or pike? No. It didn't begin with a P."

'Dorothy also recalled that her master had mentioned some special kind of fish. "Some outlandish kind of fish it was," she said.

'"A pile of – now what was it?"

'"Did he say heap or pile?" I asked.

'"I think he said pile. But there, I really can't be sure – it's so hard to remember the actual words, isn't it, Miss, especially when they don't seem to make sense. But now I come to think of it, I am pretty sure that it was a pile, and the fish began with C; but it wasn't a cod or a crayfish."

'The next part is where I am really proud of myself,' said Miss Marple, 'because, of course, I don't know anything about drugs – nasty, dangerous things I call them. I have got an old recipe of my grandmother's for tansy tea that is worth any amount of your drugs. But I knew that there were several medical volumes in the house, and in one of them there was an index of drugs. You see, my idea was that Geoffrey had taken some particular poison, and was trying to say the name of it.

'Well, I looked down the list of H's, beginning He. Nothing there that sounded likely; then I began on the P's, and almost at once I came to – what do you think?'

She looked round, postponing her moment of triumph.

'Pilocarpine. Can't you understand a man who could hardly speak trying to drag that word out? What would that sound like to a cook who had never heard the word? Wouldn't it convey the impression "pile of carp"?'

'By Jove!' said Sir Henry.

'I should never have hit upon that,' said Dr Pender.

'Most interesting,' said Mr Petherick. 'Really most interesting.'

'I turned quickly to the page indicated in the index. I read about pilocarpine and its effect on the eyes and other things that didn't seem to have any bearing on the case, but at last I came to a most significant phrase: *Has been tried with success as an antidote for atropine poisoning.*

'I can't tell you the light that dawned upon me then. I never had thought it likely that Geoffrey Denman would commit suicide. No, this new solution was not only possible, but I was absolutely sure it was the correct one, because all the pieces fitted in logically.'

'I am not going to try to guess,' said Raymond. 'Go on, Aunt Jane, and tell us what was so startlingly clear to you.'

'I don't know anything about medicine, of course,' said Miss Marple, 'but I did happen to know this, that when my eyesight was failing, the doctor ordered me drops with atropine sulphate in them. I went straight upstairs to old Mr Denman's room. I didn't beat about the bush.

'"Mr Denman," I said, "I know everything. Why did you poison your son?"

'He looked at me for a minute or two – rather a handsome old man he was, in his way – and then he burst out laughing. It was one of the most vicious laughs I have ever heard. I can assure you it made my flesh creep. I had only heard anything like it once before, when poor Mrs Jones went off her head.

'"Yes," he said, "I got even with Geoffrey. I was too clever for Geoffrey. He was going to put me away, was he? Have me shut up in an asylum? I heard them talking about it. Mabel is a good girl – Mabel stuck up for me, but I knew she wouldn't be able to stand up against Geoffrey. In the end he would have his own way; he always did. But I settled him – I settled my kind, loving son! Ha, ha! I crept down in the night. It was quite easy. Brewster was away. My dear son was asleep; he had a glass of water by the side of his bed; he always woke up in the middle of the night and drank it off. I poured it away – ha, ha! – and I emptied the bottle of eyedrops into the glass. He would wake up and swill it down before he knew what it was. There was only a tablespoonful of it – quite enough, quite enough. And so he did! They came to me in the morning and broke it to me very gently. They were afraid it would upset me. Ha! Ha! Ha! Ha! Ha!"

'Well,' said Miss Marple, 'that is the end of the story. Of course, the poor old man was put in an asylum. He wasn't really responsible for what he had done, and the truth was known, and everyone was sorry for Mabel and could not do enough to make up to her for the unjust suspicions they had had. But if it hadn't been for Geoffrey realizing what the stuff was he had swallowed and trying to get everybody to get hold of the antidote without delay, it might never have been found out. I believe there are very definite symptoms with atropine – dilated pupils of the eyes, and all that; but, of course, as I have said, Dr Rawlinson was very shortsighted, poor old man. And in the same medical book which I went on reading – and some of it was *most* interesting – it gave the symptoms of ptomaine poisoning and atropine, and they are not unlike. But I can assure you I have never seen a pile of fresh haddock without thinking of the thumb mark of St Peter.'

There was a very long pause.

'My dear friend,' said Mr Petherick. 'My very dear friend, you really are amazing.'

'I shall recommend Scotland Yard to come to you for advice,' said Sir Henry.

'Well, at all events, Aunt Jane,' said Raymond, 'there is one thing that you don't know.'

'Oh, yes, I do, dear,' said Miss Marple. 'It happened just before dinner, didn't it? When you took Joyce out to admire the sunset. It is a very favourite place, that. There by the jasmine hedge. That is where the milkman asked Annie if he could put up the banns.'

'Dash it all, Aunt Jane,' said Raymond, 'don't spoil all the romance. Joyce and I aren't like the milkman and Annie.'

'That is where you make a mistake, dear,' said Miss Marple. 'Everybody is very much alike, really. But fortunately, perhaps, they don't realize it.'

The Affair at the Bungalow

'I've thought of something,' said Jane Helier.

Her beautiful face was lit up with the confident smile of a child expecting approbation. It was a smile such as moved audiences nightly in London, and which had made the fortunes of photographers.

'It happened,' she went on carefully, 'to a friend of mine.'

Everyone made encouraging but slightly hypocritical noises. Colonel Bantry, Mrs Bantry, Sir Henry Clithering, Dr Lloyd and old Miss Marple were one and all convinced that Jane's 'friend' was Jane herself. She would have been quite incapable of remembering or taking an interest in anything affecting anyone else.

'My friend,' went on Jane, '(I won't mention her name) was an actress – a very well-known actress.'

No one expressed surprise. Sir Henry Clithering thought to himself: 'Now I wonder how many sentences it will be before she forgets to keep up the fiction, and says "I" instead of "She"?'

'My friend was on tour in the provinces – this was a year or two ago. I suppose I'd better not give the name of the place. It was a riverside town not very far from London. I'll call it –'

She paused, her brows perplexed in thought. The invention of even a simple name appeared to be too much for her. Sir Henry came to the rescue.

'Shall we call it Riverbury?' he suggested gravely.

'Oh, yes, that would do splendidly. Riverbury, I'll remember that. Well, as I say, this – my friend – was at Riverbury with her company, and a very curious thing happened.'

She puckered her brows again.

'It's very difficult,' she said plaintively, 'to say just what you want. One gets things mixed up and tells the wrong thing first.'

'You're doing it beautifully,' said Dr Lloyd encouragingly. 'Go on.'

'Well, this curious thing happened. My friend was sent for to the police station. And she went. It seemed there had been a burglary at a riverside bungalow and they'd arrested a young man, and he told a very odd story. And so they sent for her.'

'She'd never been to a police station before, but they were very nice to her – very nice indeed.'

'They would be, I'm sure,' said Sir Henry.

'The sergeant – I think it was a sergeant – or it may have been an inspector – gave her a chair and explained things, and of course I saw at once that it was some mistake –'

'Aha,' thought Sir Henry. 'I. Here we are. I thought as much.'

'My friend said so,' continued Jane, serenely unconscious of her self-betrayal. 'She explained she had been rehearsing with her understudy at the hotel and that she'd never even heard of this Mr Faulkener. And the sergeant said, "Miss Hel –"'

She stopped and flushed.

'Miss Helman,' suggested Sir Henry with a twinkle.

'Yes – yes, that would do. Thank you. He said, "Well, Miss Helman, I felt it must be some mistake, knowing that you were stopping at the Bridge Hotel," and he said would I have any objection to confronting – or was it being confronted? I can't remember.'

'It doesn't really matter,' said Sir Henry reassuringly.

'Anyway, with the young man. So I said, "Of course not."

And they brought him and said, "This is Miss Helier," and – Oh!' Jane broke off open-mouthed.

'Never mind, my dear,' said Miss Marple consolingly. 'We were bound to guess, you know. And you haven't given us the name of the place or anything that really matters.'

'Well,' said Jane. 'I did mean to tell it as though it happened to someone else. But it *is* difficult, isn't it! I mean one forgets so.'

Everyone assured her that it was very difficult, and soothed and reassured, she went on with her slightly involved narrative.

'He was a nice-looking man – quite a nice-looking man. Young, with reddish hair. His mouth just opened when he saw me. And the sergeant said, "Is this the lady?" And he said, "No, indeed it isn't. What an ass I have been." And I smiled at him and said it didn't matter.'

'I can picture the scene,' said Sir Henry.

Jane Helier frowned.

'Let me see – how had I better go on?'

'Supposing you tell us what it was all about, dear,' said Miss Marple, so mildly that no one could suspect her of irony. 'I mean what the young man's mistake was, and about the burglary.'

'Oh, yes,' said Jane. 'Well, you see, this young man – Leslie Faulkener, his name was – had written a play. He'd written several plays, as a matter of fact, though none of them had ever been taken. And he had sent this particular play to me to read. I didn't know about it, because of course I have hundreds of plays sent to me and I read very few of them myself – only the ones I know something about. Anyway, there it was, and it seems that Mr Faulkener got a letter from me – only it turned out not to be really from me – you understand –'

She paused anxiously, and they assured her that they understood.

'Saying that I'd read the play, and liked it very much and would he come down and talk it over with me. And it gave the address – The Bungalow, Riverbury. So Mr Faulkener was frightfully pleased and he came down and arrived at this place – The Bungalow. A parlourmaid opened the door, and he asked for Miss Helier, and she said Miss Helier was in and expecting him and showed him into the drawing-room, and there a woman came to him. And he accepted her as me as a matter of course – which seems queer because after all he had seen me act and my photographs are very well known, aren't they?'

'Over the length and breadth of England,' said Mrs Bantry promptly. 'But there's often a lot of difference between a photograph and its original, my dear Jane. And there's a great deal of difference between behind the footlights and off the stage. It's not every actress who stands the test as well as you do, remember.'

'Well,' said Jane slightly mollified, 'that may be so. Anyway, he described this woman as tall and fair with big blue eyes and very good-looking, so I suppose it must have been near enough. He certainly had no suspicions. She sat down and began talking about his play and said she was anxious to do it. Whilst they were talking cocktails were brought in and Mr Faulkener had one as a matter of course. Well – that's all he remembers – having this cocktail. When he woke up, or came to himself, or whatever you call it – he was lying out in the road, by the hedge, of course, so that there would be no danger of his being run over. He felt very queer and shaky – so much so that he just got up and staggered along the road not quite knowing where he was going. He said if he'd had his senses about him he'd have gone back to The Bungalow and tried to find out what had happened. But he felt just stupid and mazed and walked along without quite knowing what he was doing. He was just more or less coming to himself when the police arrested him.'

'Why did the police arrest him?' asked Dr Lloyd.

'Oh! didn't I tell you?' said Jane opening her eyes very wide. 'How very stupid I am. The burglary.'

'You mentioned a burglary – but you didn't say where or what or why,' said Mrs Bantry.

'Well, this bungalow – the one he went to, of course – it wasn't mine at all. It belonged to a man whose name was –'

Again Jane furrowed her brows.

'Do you want me to be godfather again?' asked Sir Henry. 'Pseudonyms supplied free of charge. Describe the tenant and I'll do the naming.'

'It was taken by a rich city man – a knight.'

'Sir Herman Cohen,' suggested Sir Henry.

'That will do beautifully. He took it for a lady – she was the wife of an actor, and she was also an actress herself.'

'We'll call the actor Claud Leason,' said Sir Henry, 'and the lady would be known by her stage name, I suppose, so we'll call her Miss Mary Kerr.'

'I think you're awfully clever,' said Jane. 'I don't know how you think of these things so easily. Well, you see this was a sort of week-end cottage for Sir Herman – did you say Herman? – and the lady. And, of course, his wife knew nothing about it.'

'Which is so often the case,' said Sir Henry.

'And he'd given this actress woman a good deal of jewellery including some very fine emeralds.'

'Ah!' said Dr Lloyd. 'Now we're getting at it.'

'This jewellery was at the bungalow, just locked up in a jewel case. The police said it was very careless – anyone might have taken it.'

'You see, Dolly,' said Colonel Bantry. 'What do I always tell you?'

'Well, in my experience,' said Mrs Bantry, 'it's always the people who are so dreadfully careful who lose things. I don't lock mine up in a jewel case – I keep it in a drawer loose, under my stockings. I dare say if – what's her name? – Mary Kerr had done the same, it would never have been stolen.'

'It would,' said Jane, 'because all the drawers were burst open, and the contents strewn about.'

'Then they weren't really looking for jewels,' said Mrs Bantry. 'They were looking for secret papers. That's what always happens in books.'

'I don't know about secret papers,' said Jane doubtfully. 'I never heard of any.'

'Don't be distracted, Miss Helier,' said Colonel Bantry. 'Dolly's wild red-herrings are not to be taken seriously.'

'About the burglary,' said Sir Henry.

'Yes. Well, the police were rung up by someone who said she was Miss Mary Kerr. She said the bungalow had been burgled and described a young man with red hair who had called there that morning. Her maid had thought there was something odd about him and had refused him admittance, but later they had seen him getting out through a window. She described the man so accurately that the police arrested him only an hour later and then he told his story and showed them the letter from me. And as I told you, they fetched me and when he saw me he said what I told you – that it hadn't been me at all!'

'A very curious story,' said Dr Lloyd. 'Did Mr Faulkener know this Miss Kerr?'

'No, he didn't – or he said he didn't. But I haven't told you the most curious part yet. The police went to the bungalow of course, and they found everything as described – drawers pulled out and jewels gone, but the whole place was empty. It wasn't till some hours later that Mary Kerr came back, and when she did she said she'd never rung them up at all and this was the first she'd heard of it. It seemed that she had had a wire that morning from a manager offering her a most important part and making an appointment, so she had naturally rushed up to town to keep it. When she got there, she found that the whole thing was a hoax. No telegram had ever been sent.'

'A common enough ruse to get her out of the way,' commented Sir Henry. 'What about the servants?'

'The same sort of thing happened there. There was only one, and she was rung up on the telephone – apparently by Mary Kerr, who said she had left a most important thing behind. She directed the maid to bring up a certain handbag which was in the drawer of her bedroom. She was to catch the first train. The maid did so, of course locking up the house; but when she arrived at Miss Kerr's club, where she had been told to meet her mistress, she waited there in vain.'

'H'm,' said Sir Henry. 'I begin to see. The house was left empty, and to make an entry by one of the windows would present few difficulties, I should imagine. But I don't quite see where Mr Faulkener comes in. Who did ring up the police, if it wasn't Miss Kerr?'

'That's what nobody knew or ever found out.'

'Curious,' said Sir Henry. 'Did the young man turn out to be genuinely the person he said he was?'

'Oh, yes, that part of it was all right. He'd even got the letter which was supposed to be written by me. It wasn't the least bit like my handwriting – but then, of course, he couldn't be supposed to know that.'

'Well, let's state the position clearly,' said Sir Henry. 'Correct me if I go wrong. The lady and the maid are decoyed from the house. This young man is decoyed down there by means of a bogus letter – colour being lent to this last by the fact that you actually are performing at Riverbury that week. The young man is doped, and the police are rung up and have their suspicions directed against him. A burglary actually has taken place. I presume the jewels were taken?'

'Oh, yes.'

'Were they ever recovered?'

'No, never. I think, as a matter of fact, Sir Herman tried to hush things up all he knew how. But he couldn't manage it, and I rather fancy his wife started divorce proceedings in consequence. Still, I don't really know about that.'

'What happened to Mr Leslie Faulkener?'

'He was released in the end. The police said they hadn't really got enough against him. Don't you think the whole thing was rather odd?'

'Distinctly odd. The first question is whose story to believe? In telling it, Miss Helier, I noticed that you incline towards believing Mr Faulkener. Have you any reason for doing so beyond your own instinct in the matter?'

'No-no,' said Jane unwillingly. 'I suppose I haven't. But he was so very nice, and so apologetic for having mistaken anyone else for me, that I feel sure he *must* have been telling the truth.'

'I see,' said Sir Henry smiling. 'But you must admit that he could have invented the story quite easily. He could write the letter purporting to be from you himself. He could also dope himself after successfully committing the burglary. But I confess I don't see where the *point* of all that would be. Easier to enter the house, help himself, and disappear quietly – unless just possibly he was observed by someone in the neighbour-hood and knew himself to have been observed. Then he might hastily concoct this plan for diverting suspicion from himself and accounting for his presence in the neighbourhood.'

'Was he well off?' asked Miss Marple.

'I don't think so,' said Jane. 'No, I believe he was rather hard up.'

'The whole thing seems curious,' said Dr Lloyd. 'I must confess that if we accept the young man's story as true, it seems to make the case very much more difficult. Why should the unknown woman who pretended to be Miss Helier drag this unknown man into the affair? Why should she stage such an elaborate comedy?'

'Tell me, Jane,' said Mrs Bantry. 'Did young Faulkener ever come face to face with Mary Kerr at any stage of the proceedings?'

'I don't quite know,' said Jane slowly, as she puzzled her brows in remembrance.

'Because if he didn't the case is solved!' said Mrs Bantry. 'I'm sure I'm right. What is easier than to pretend you're called up to town? You telephone to your maid from Paddington or whatever station you arrive at, and as she comes up to town, you go down again. The young man calls by appointment, he's doped, you set the stage for the burglary, overdoing it as much as possible. You telephone the police, give a description of your scapegoat, and off you go to town again. Then you arrive home by a later train and do the surprised innocent.'

'But why should she steal her own jewels, Dolly?'

'They always do,' said Mrs Bantry. 'And anyway, I can think of hundreds of reasons. She may have wanted money at once – old Sir Herman wouldn't give her the cash, perhaps, so she pretends the jewels are stolen and then sells them secretly. Or she may have been being blackmailed by someone who threatened to tell her husband or Sir Herman's wife. Or she may have already sold the jewels and Sir Herman was getting ratty and asking to see them, so she had to do something about it. That's done a good deal in books. Or perhaps she was going to have them reset and she'd got paste replicas. Or – here's a very good idea – and not so much done in books – she pretends they are stolen, gets in an awful state and he gives her a fresh lot. So she gets two lots instead of one. That kind of woman, I am sure, is most frightfully artful.'

'You are clever, Dolly,' said Jane admiringly. 'I never thought of that.'

'You may be clever, but she doesn't say you're right,' said Colonel Bantry. 'I incline to suspicion of the city gentleman. He'd know the sort of telegram to get the lady out of the way, and he could manage the rest easily enough with the help of a new lady friend. Nobody seems to have thought of asking *him* for an alibi.'

'What do you think, Miss Marple?' asked Jane, turning towards the old lady who had sat silent, a puzzled frown on her face.

'My dear, I really don't know what to say. Sir Henry will laugh, but I recall no village parallel to help me this time. Of course there are several questions that suggest themselves. For instance, the servant question. In – ahem – an irregular *ménage* of the kind you describe, the servant employed would doubtless be perfectly aware of the state of things, and a really nice girl would not take such a place – her mother wouldn't let her for a minute. So I think we can assume that the maid was *not* a really trustworthy character. She may have been in league with the thieves. She would leave the house open for them and actually go to London as though sure of the pretence telephone message so as to divert suspicion from herself. I must confess that that seems the most probable solution. Only if ordinary thieves were concerned it seems very odd. It seems to argue more knowledge than a maidservant was likely to have.'

Miss Marple paused and then went on dreamily:

'I can't help feeling that there was some – well, what I must describe as personal feeling about the whole thing. Supposing somebody had a spite, for instance? A young actress that he hadn't treated well? Don't you think that that would explain things better? A deliberate attempt to get him into trouble. That's what it looks like. And yet – that's not entirely satisfactory . . .'

'Why, doctor, you haven't said anything,' said Jane. 'I'd forgotten you.'

'I'm always getting forgotten,' said the grizzled doctor sadly. 'I must have a very inconspicuous personality.'

'Oh, no!' said Jane. 'Do tell us what you think.'

'I'm rather in the position of agreeing with everyone's solutions – and yet with none of them. I myself have a far-fetched and probably totally erroneous theory that the wife may have had something to do with it. Sir Herman's wife, I mean. I've no grounds for thinking so, only you would be surprised if you knew the extraordinary – really *very* extraordinary – things that a wronged wife will take it into her head to do.'

'Oh! Dr Lloyd,' cried Miss Marple excitedly. 'How clever of you. And I never thought of poor Mrs Pebmarsh.'

Jane stared at her.

'Mrs Pebmarsh? Who is Mrs Pebmarsh?'

'Well –' Miss Marple hesitated. 'I don't know that she really comes in. She's a laundress. And she stole an opal pin that was pinned into a blouse and put it in another woman's house.'

Jane looked more fogged than ever.

'And that makes it all perfectly clear to you, Miss Marple?' said Sir Henry, with his twinkle.

But to his surprise Miss Marple shook her head.

'No, I'm afraid it doesn't. I must confess myself completely at a loss. What I do realize is that women must stick together – one should, in an emergency, stand by one's own sex. I think that's the moral of the story Miss Helier has told us.'

'I must confess that that particular ethical significance of the mystery has escaped me,' said Sir Henry gravely. 'Perhaps I shall see the significance of your point more clearly when Miss Helier has revealed the solution.'

'Eh?' said Jane looking rather bewildered.

'I was observing that, in childish language, we "give it up". You and you alone, Miss Helier, have had the high honour of presenting such an absolutely baffling mystery that even Miss Marple has to confess herself defeated.'

'You all give it up?' asked Jane.

'Yes.' After a minute's silence during which he waited for

the others to speak, Sir Henry constituted himself spokesman once more. 'That is to say we stand or fall by the sketchy solutions we have tentatively advanced. One each for the mere men, two for Miss Marple, and a round dozen from Mrs B.'

'It was not a dozen,' said Mrs Bantry. 'They were variations on a main theme. And how often am I to tell you that I will *not* be called Mrs B?'

'So you all give it up,' said Jane thoughtfully. 'That's very interesting.'

She leaned back in her chair and began to polish her nails rather absent-mindedly.

'Well,' said Mrs Bantry. 'Come on, Jane. What is the solution?'

'The solution?'

'Yes. What really happened?'

Jane stared at her.

'I haven't the least idea.'

'*What?*'

'I've always wondered. I thought you were all so clever one of you would be able to tell *me*.'

Everybody harboured feelings of annoyance. It was all very well for Jane to be so beautiful – but at this moment everyone felt that stupidity could be carried too far. Even the most transcendent loveliness could not excuse it.

'You mean the truth was never discovered?' said Sir Henry.

'No. That's why, as I say, I did think you would be able to tell *me*.'

Jane sounded injured. It was plain that she felt she had a grievance.

'Well – I'm – I'm –' said Colonel Bantry, words failing him.

'You are the most aggravating girl, Jane,' said his wife. 'Anyway, I'm sure and always will be that I was right. If you just tell us the proper names of the people, I shall be *quite* sure.'

'I don't think I could do that,' said Jane slowly.

'No, dear,' said Miss Marple. 'Miss Helier couldn't do that.'

'Of course she could,' said Mrs Bantry. 'Don't be so high-minded, Jane. We older folk must have a bit of scandal. At any rate tell us who the city magnate was.'

But Jane shook her head, and Miss Marple, in her old-fashioned way, continued to support the girl.

'It must have been a very distressing business,' she said.

'No,' said Jane truthfully. 'I think – I think I rather enjoyed it.'

'Well, perhaps you did,' said Miss Marple. 'I suppose it was a break in the monotony. What play were you acting in?'

'*Smith.*'

'Oh, yes. That's one of Mr Somerset Maugham's, isn't it? All his are very clever, I think. I've seen them nearly all.'

'You're reviving it to go on tour next autumn, aren't you?' asked Mrs Bantry.

Jane nodded.

'Well,' said Miss Marple rising. 'I must go home. Such late hours! But we've had a very entertaining evening. Most unusually so. I think Miss Helier's story wins the prize. Don't you agree?'

'I'm sorry you're angry with me,' said Jane. 'About not knowing the end, I mean. I suppose I should have said so sooner.'

Her tone sounded wistful. Dr Lloyd rose gallantly to the occasion.

'My dear young lady, why should you? You gave us a very pretty problem to sharpen our wits on. I am only sorry we could none of us solve it convincingly.'

'Speak for yourself,' said Mrs Bantry. 'I *did* solve it. I'm convinced I am right.'

'Do you know, I really believe you are,' said Jane. 'What you said sounded so probable.'

'Which of her seven solutions do you refer to?' asked Sir Henry teasingly.

Dr Lloyd gallantly assisted Miss Marple to put on her

40

galoshes. 'Just in case,' as the old lady explained. The doctor was to be her escort to her old-world cottage. Wrapped in several woollen shawls, Miss Marple wished everyone good night once more. She came to Jane Helier last and leaning forward, she murmured something in the actress's ear. A startled 'Oh!' burst from Jane – so loud as to cause the others to turn their heads.

Smiling and nodding, Miss Marple made her exit, Jane Helier staring after her.

'Are you coming to bed, Jane?' asked Mrs Bantry. 'What's the matter with you? You're staring as though you'd seen a ghost.'

With a deep sigh Jane came to herself, shed a beautiful and bewildering smile on the two men and followed her hostess up the staircase. Mrs Bantry came into the girl's room with her.

'Your fire's nearly out,' said Mrs Bantry, giving it a vicious and ineffectual poke. 'They can't have made it up properly. How stupid housemaids are. Still, I suppose we are rather late tonight. Why, it's actually past one o'clock!'

'Do you think there are many people like her?' asked Jane Helier.

She was sitting on the side of the bed apparently wrapped in thought.

'Like the housemaid?'

'No. Like that funny old woman – what's her name – Marple?'

'Oh! I don't know. I suppose she's a fairly common type in a small village.'

'Oh dear,' said Jane. 'I don't know what to do.'

She sighed deeply.

'What's the matter?'

'I'm worried.'

'What about?'

'Dolly,' Jane Helier was portentously solemn. 'Do you know what that queer old lady whispered to me before she went out of the door tonight?'

'No. What?'

'She said: "*I shouldn't do it if I were you, my dear. Never put yourself too much in another woman's power, even if you do think she's your friend at the moment.*" You know, Dolly, that's awfully true.'

'The maxim? Yes, perhaps it is. But I don't see the application.'

'I suppose you can't ever really trust a woman. And I should be in her power. I never thought of that.'

'What woman are you talking about?'

'Netta Greene, my understudy.'

'What on earth does Miss Marple know about your understudy?'

'I suppose she guessed – but I can't see how.'

'Jane, will you kindly tell me at once what you are talking about?'

'The story. The one I told. Oh, Dolly, that woman, you know – the one that took Claud from me?'

Mrs Bantry nodded, casting her mind back rapidly to the first of Jane's unfortunate marriages – to Claud Averbury, the actor.

'He married her; and I could have told him how it would be. Claud doesn't know, but she's carrying on with Sir Joseph Salmon – week-ends with him at the bungalow I told you about. I wanted her shown up – I would like everyone to know the sort of woman she was. And you see, with a burglary, everything would be bound to come out.'

'Jane!' gasped Mrs Bantry. 'Did *you* engineer this story you've been telling us?'

Jane nodded.

'That's why I chose *Smith*. I wear parlourmaid's kit in it, you know. So I should have it handy. And when they sent for me to the police station it's the easiest thing in the world to say I was rehearsing my part with my understudy at the hotel. Really, of course, we would be at the bungalow. I just have to open the door and bring in the cocktails, and Netta to pretend to be me. He'd never see *her* again, of course, so there would be no fear of his recognizing her. And I can make myself look quite different as a parlourmaid; and besides, one doesn't look at parlourmaids as though they were people. We planned to drag him out into the road afterwards, bag the jewel case, telephone the police and get back to the hotel. I shouldn't like the poor young man to suffer, but Sir Henry didn't seem to think he would, did he? And she'd be in the papers and everything – and Claud would see what she was really like.'

Mrs Bantry sat down and groaned.

'Oh! my poor head. And all the time – Jane Helier, you deceitful girl! Telling us that story the way you did!'

'I *am* a good actress,' said Jane complacently. 'I always have been, whatever people choose to say. I didn't give myself away once, did I?'

'Miss Marple was right,' murmured Mrs Bantry. 'The personal element. Oh, yes, the personal element. Jane, my good child, do you realize that theft is theft, and you might have been sent to prison?'

'Well, none of you guessed,' said Jane. 'Except Miss Marple.' The worried expression returned to her face. 'Dolly, do you *really* think there are many like her?'

'Frankly, I don't,' said Mrs Bantry.

Jane sighed again.

'Still, one had better not risk it. And of course I should be in Netta's power – that's true enough. She might turn against me or blackmail me or anything. She helped me think out the details and she professed to be devoted to me, but one never *does* know with women. No, I think Miss Marple was right. I had better not risk it.'

'But, my dear, you have risked it.'

'Oh, no.' Jane opened her blue eyes very wide. 'Don't you

understand? *None of this has happened yet*! I was – well, trying it on the dog, so to speak.'

'I don't profess to understand your theatrical slang,' said Mrs Bantry with dignity. 'Do you mean this is a future project – not a past deed?'

'I was going to do it this autumn – in September. I don't know what to do now.'

'And Jane Marple guessed – actually guessed the truth and never told us,' said Mrs Bantry wrathfully.

'I think that was why she said that – about women sticking together. She wouldn't give me away before the men. That was nice of her. I don't mind *your* knowing, Dolly.'

'Well, give the idea up, Jane. I beg of you.'

'I think I shall,' murmured Miss Helier. 'There might be other Miss Marples . . .'

The Affair at the Victory Ball

I

Pure chance led my friend Hercule Poirot, formerly chief of the Belgian force, to be connected with the Styles Case. His success brought him notoriety, and he decided to devote himself to the solving of problems in crime. Having been wounded on the Somme and invalided out of the Army, I finally took up my quarters with him in London. Since I have a first-hand knowledge of most of his cases, it has been suggested to me that I select some of the most interesting and place them on record. In doing so, I feel that I cannot do better than begin with that strange tangle which aroused such widespread public interest at the time. I refer to the affair at the Victory Ball.

Although perhaps it is not so fully demonstrative of Poirot's peculiar methods as some of the more obscure cases, its sensational features, the well-known people involved, and the tremendous publicity given it by the Press, make it stand out as a *cause célèbre* and I have long felt that it is only fitting that Poirot's connection with the solution should be given to the world.

It was a fine morning in spring, and we were sitting in Poirot's rooms. My little friend, neat and dapper as ever, his egg-shaped head tilted on one side, was delicately applying a new pomade to his moustache. A certain harmless vanity was a characteristic of Poirot's and fell into line with his general love of order and method. The *Daily Newsmonger*, which I had been reading, had slipped to the floor, and I was deep in a brown study when Poirot's voice recalled me.

'Of what are you thinking so deeply, *mon ami*?'

'To tell you the truth,' I replied, 'I was puzzling over this unaccountable affair at the Victory Ball. The papers are full of it.' I tapped the sheet with my finger as I spoke.

'Yes?'

'The more one reads of it, the more shrouded in mystery the whole thing becomes!' I warmed to my subject. 'Who killed Lord Cronshaw? Was Coco Courtenay's death on the same night a mere coincidence? Was it an accident? Or did she deliberately take an overdose of cocaine?' I stopped, and then added dramatically: 'These are the questions I ask myself.'

Poirot, somewhat to my annoyance, did not play up. He was peering into the glass, and merely murmured: 'Decidedly, this new pomade, it is a marvel for the moustaches!' Catching my eye, however, he added hastily: 'Quite so – and how do you reply to your questions?'

But before I could answer, the door opened, and our landlady announced Inspector Japp.

The Scotland Yard man was an old friend of ours and we greeted him warmly.

'Ah, my good Japp,' cried Poirot, 'and what brings you to see us?'

'Well, Monsieur Poirot,' said Japp, seating himself and nodding to me, 'I'm on a case that strikes me as being very much in your line, and I came along to know whether you'd care to have a finger in the pie?'

Poirot had a good opinion of Japp's abilities, though deploring his lamentable lack of method, but I, for my part, considered that the detective's highest talent lay in the gentle art of seeking favours under the guise of conferring them!

'It's the Victory Ball,' said Japp persuasively. 'Come, now, you'd like to have a hand in that.'

Poirot smiled at me.

'My friend Hastings would, at all events. He was just holding forth on the subject, *n'est-ce pas, mon ami*?'

'Well, sir,' said Japp condescendingly, 'you shall be in it too. I can tell you, it's something of a feather in your cap to have inside knowledge of a case like this. Well, here's to business. You know the main facts of the case, I suppose, Monsieur Poirot?'

'From the papers only – and the imagination of the journalist is sometimes misleading. Recount the whole story to me.'

Japp crossed his legs comfortably and began.

'As all the world and his wife knows, on Tuesday last a grand Victory Ball was held. Every twopenny-halfpenny hop calls itself that nowadays, but this was the real thing, held at the Colossus Hall, and all London at it – including young Lord Cronshaw and his party.'

'His *dossier*?' interrupted Poirot. 'I should say his bioscope – no, how do you call it – biograph?'

'Viscount Cronshaw was the fifth viscount, twenty-five years of age, rich, unmarried, and very fond of the theatrical world. There were rumours of his being engaged to Miss Courtenay of the Albany Theatre, who was known to her friends as "Coco" and who was, by all accounts, a very fascinating young lady.'

'Good. *Continuez!*'

'Lord Cronshaw's party consisted of six people: he himself, his uncle, the Honourable Eustace Beltane, a pretty American widow, Mrs Mallaby, a young actor, Chris Davidson, his wife, and last but not least, Miss Coco Courtenay. It was a fancy dress ball, as you know, and the Cronshaw party represented the old Italian Comedy – whatever that may be.'

'The *Commedia dell'Arte*,' murmured Poirot. 'I know.'

47

'Anyway, the costumes were copied from a set of china figurines forming part of Eustace Beltane's collection. Lord Cronshaw was Harlequin; Beltane was Punchinello; Mrs Mallaby matched him as Pulcinella; the Davidsons were Pierrot and Pierette; and Miss Courtenay, of course, was Columbine. Now, quite early in the evening it was apparent that there was something wrong. Lord Cronshaw was moody and strange in his manner. When the party met together for supper in a small private room engaged by the host, everyone noticed that he and Miss Courtenay were no longer on speaking terms. She had obviously been crying, and seemed on the verge of hysterics. The meal was an uncomfortable one, and as they all left the supper-room, she turned to Chris Davidson and requested him audibly to take her home, as she was "sick of the ball". The young actor hesitated, glancing at Lord Cronshaw, and finally drew them both back to the supper-room.

'But all his efforts to secure a reconciliation were unavailing, and he accordingly got a taxi and escorted the now weeping Miss Courtenay back to her flat. Although obviously very much upset, she did not confide in him, merely reiterating again and again that she would "make old Cronch sorry for this!" That is the only hint we have that her death might not have been accidental, and it's precious little to go upon. By the time Davidson had quieted her down somewhat, it was too late to return to the Colossus Hall, and Davidson accordingly went straight home to his flat in Chelsea, where his wife arrived shortly afterwards, bearing the news of the terrible tragedy that had occurred after his departure.

'Lord Cronshaw, it seems, became more and more moody as the ball went on. He kept away from his party, and they hardly saw him during the rest of the evening. It was about one-thirty a.m., just before the grand cotillion when everyone was to unmask, that Captain Digby, a brother officer who knew his disguise, noticed him standing in a box gazing down on the scene.

'"Hullo, Cronch!" he called. "Come down and be sociable! What are you moping about up there for like a boiled owl? Come along; there's a good old rag coming on now."

'"Right!" responded Cronshaw. "Wait for me, or I'll never find you in the crowd."

'He turned and left the box as he spoke. Captain Digby, who had Mrs Davidson with him, waited. The minutes passed, but Lord Cronshaw did not appear. Finally Digby grew impatient.

'"Does the fellow think we're going to wait all night for him?" he exclaimed.

'At that moment Mrs Mallaby joined them, and they explained the situation.

'"Say, now," cried the pretty widow vivaciously, "he's like a bear with a sore head tonight. Let's go right away and rout him out."

'The search commenced, but met with no success until it occurred to Mrs Mallaby that he might possibly be found in the room where they had supped an hour earlier. They made their way there. What a sight met their eyes! There was Harlequin, sure enough, but stretched on the ground with a table-knife in his heart!'

Japp stopped, and Poirot nodded, and said with the relish of the specialist: '*Une belle affaire*! And there was no clue as to the perpetrator of the deed? But how should there be!'

'Well,' continued the inspector, 'you know the rest. The tragedy was a double one. Next day there were headlines in all the papers, and a brief statement to the effect that Miss Courtenay, the popular actress, had been discovered dead in her bed, and that her death was due to an overdose of cocaine. Now, was it accident or suicide? Her maid, who was called upon to give evidence, admitted that Miss Courtenay was a confirmed taker of the drug, and a verdict of accidental death was returned. Nevertheless we can't leave the possibility of suicide out of account. Her death is particularly unfortunate, since it leaves us no clue now to the cause of the quarrel the preceding night. By the way, a small enamel box was found on the dead man. It had *Coco* written across it in diamonds, and was half full of cocaine. It was identified by Miss Courtenay's maid as belonging to her mistress, who nearly always carried it about with her, since it contained her supply of the drug to which she was fast becoming a slave.'

'Was Lord Cronshaw himself addicted to the drug?'

'Very far from it. He held unusually strong views on the subject of dope.'

Poirot nodded thoughtfully.

'But since the box was in his possession, he knew that Miss Courtenay took cocaine. Suggestive, that, is it not, my good Japp?'

'Ah!' said Japp rather vaguely.

I smiled.

'Well,' said Japp, 'that's the case. What do you think of it?'

'You found no clue of any kind that has not been reported?'

'Yes, there was this.' Japp took a small object from his pocket and handed it over to Poirot. It was a small pompon of emerald green silk, with some ragged threads hanging from it, as though it had been wrenched violently away.

'We found it in the dead man's hand, which was tightly clenched over it,' explained the inspector.

Poirot handed it back without any comment and asked: 'Had Lord Cronshaw any enemies?'

'None that anyone knows of. He seemed a popular young fellow.'

'Who benefits by his death?'

'His uncle, the Honourable Eustace Beltane, comes into the title and estates. There are one or two suspicious facts against him. Several people declare that they heard a violent altercation going on in the little supper-room, and that Eustace Beltane was one of the disputants. You see, the table-knife being snatched up off the table would fit in with the murder being done in the heat of a quarrel.'

'What does Mr Beltane say about the matter?'

'Declares one of the waiters was the worse for liquor, and that he was giving him a dressing down. Also that it was nearer to one than half past. You see, Captain Digby's evidence fixes the time pretty accurately. Only about ten minutes elapsed between his speaking to Cronshaw and the finding of the body.'

'And in any case I suppose Mr Beltane, as Punchinello, was wearing a hump and a ruffle?'

'I don't know the exact details of the costumes,' said Japp, looking curiously at Poirot. 'And anyway, I don't quite see what that has got to do with it?'

'No?' There was a hint of mockery in Poirot's smile. He continued quietly, his eyes shining with the green light I had learned to recognize so well: 'There was a curtain in this little supper-room, was there not?'

'Yes, but –'

'With a space behind it sufficient to conceal a man?'

'Yes – in fact, there's a small recess, but how you knew about it – you haven't been to the place, have you, Monsieur Poirot?'

'No, my good Japp, I supplied the curtain from my brain. Without it, the drama is not reasonable. And always one must be reasonable. But tell me, did they not send for a doctor?'

'At once, of course. But there was nothing to be done. Death must have been instantaneous.'

Poirot nodded rather impatiently.

'Yes, yes, I understand. This doctor, now, he gave evidence at the inquest?'

'Yes.'

'Did he say nothing of any unusual symptom – was there nothing about the appearance of the body which struck him as being abnormal?'

Japp stared hard at the little man.

'Yes, Monsieur Poirot. I don't know what you're getting at, but he did mention that there was a tension and stiffness about the limbs which he was quite at a loss to account for.'

'Aha!' said Poirot. 'Aha! *Mon Dieu!* Japp, that gives one to think, does it not?'

I saw that it had certainly not given Japp to think.

'If you're thinking of poison, monsieur, who on earth would poison a man first and then stick a knife into him?'

'In truth that would be ridiculous,' agreed Poirot placidly.

'Now is there anything you want to see, monsieur? If you'd like to examine the room where the body was found –'

Poirot waved his hand.

'Not in the least. You have told me the only thing that interests me – Lord Cronshaw's views on the subject of drug taking.'

'Then there's nothing you want to see?'

'Just one thing.'

'What is that?'

'The set of china figures from which the costumes were copied.'

Japp stared.

'Well, you're a funny one!'

'You can manage that for me?'

'Come round to Berkeley Square now if you like. Mr Beltane – or His Lordship, as I should say now – won't object.'

II

We set off at once in a taxi. The new Lord Cronshaw was not at home, but at Japp's request we were shown into the 'china room', where the gems of the collection were kept. Japp looked round him rather helplessly.

'I don't see how you'll ever find the ones you want, monsieur.'

But Poirot had already drawn a chair in front of the mantelpiece and was hopping up upon it like a nimble robin. Above the mirror, on a small shelf to themselves, stood six china figures. Poirot examined them minutely, making a few comments to us as he did so.

'*Les voilà!* The old Italian Comedy. Three pairs! Harlequin and Columbine, Pierrot and Pierrette – very dainty in white and green – and Punchinello and Pulcinella in mauve and yellow. Very elaborate, the costume of Punchinello – ruffles and frills, a hump, a high hat. Yes, as I thought, very elaborate.'

He replaced the figures carefully, and jumped down.

Japp looked unsatisfied, but as Poirot had clearly no intention of explaining anything, the detective put the best face he could upon the matter. As we were preparing to leave, the master of the house came in, and Japp performed the necessary introductions.

The sixth Viscount Cronshaw was a man of about fifty, suave in manner, with a handsome, dissolute face. Evidently an elderly roué, with the languid manner of a poseur. I took an instant dislike to him. He greeted us graciously enough, declaring he had heard great accounts of Poirot's skill, and placing himself at our disposal in every way.

'The police are doing all they can, I know,' Poirot said.

'But I much fear the mystery of my nephew's death will never be cleared up. The whole thing seems utterly mysterious.'

Poirot was watching him keenly. 'Your nephew had no enemies that you know of?'

'None whatever. I am sure of that.' He paused, and then went on: 'If there are any questions you would like to ask –'

'Only one.' Poirot's voice was serious. 'The costumes – they were reproduced *exactly* from your figurines?'

'To the smallest detail.'

'Thank you, milor'. That is all I wanted to be sure of. I wish you good day.'

'And what next?' inquired Japp as we hurried down the street. 'I've got to report at the Yard, you know.'

'*Bien*! I will not detain you. I have one other little matter to attend to, and then –'

'Yes?'

'The case will be complete.'

'What? You don't mean it! You know who killed Lord Cronshaw?'

'*Parfaitement.*'

'Who was it? Eustace Beltane?'

'Ah, *mon ami*, you know my little weakness! Always I have a desire to keep the threads in my own hands up to the last minute. But have no fear. I will reveal all when the time comes. I want no credit – the affair shall be yours, on the condition that you permit me to play out the *dénouement* my own way.'

'That's fair enough,' said Japp. 'That is, if the *dénouement* ever comes! But I say, you *are* an oyster, aren't you?' Poirot smiled. 'Well, so long. I'm off to the Yard.'

He strode off down the street, and Poirot hailed a passing taxi.

'Where are we going now?' I asked in lively curiosity.

'To Chelsea to see the Davidsons.'

He gave the address to the driver.

'What do you think of the new Lord Cronshaw?' I asked.

'What says my good friend Hastings?'

'I distrust him instinctively.'

'You think he is the "wicked uncle" of the story-books, eh?'

'Don't you?'

'Me, I think he was most amiable towards us,' said Poirot noncommittally.

'Because he had his reasons!'

Poirot looked at me, shook his head sadly, and murmured something that sounded like: 'No method.'

III

The Davidsons lived on the third floor of a block of 'mansion' flats. Mr Davidson was out, we were told, but Mrs Davidson was at home. We were ushered into a long, low room with garish Oriental hangings. The air felt close and oppressive, and there was an overpowering fragrance of joss-sticks. Mrs Davidson came to us almost immediately, a small, fair creature whose fragility would have seemed pathetic and appealing had it not been for the rather shrewd and calculating gleam in her light blue eyes.

Poirot explained our connection with the case, and she shook her head sadly.

'Poor Cronch – and poor Coco too! We were both so fond of her, and her death has been a terrible grief to us. What is it you want to ask me? Must I really go over all that dreadful evening again?'

'Oh, madame, believe me, I would not harass your feelings unnecessarily. Indeed, Inspector Japp has told me all that is needful. I only wish to see the costume you wore at the ball that night.'

The lady looked somewhat surprised, and Poirot continued smoothly: 'You comprehend, madame, that I work on the system of my country. There we always "reconstruct" the crime. It is possible that I may have an actual *représentation*, and if so, you understand, the costumes would be important.'

Mrs Davidson still looked a bit doubtful.

'I've heard of reconstructing a crime, of course,' she said. 'But I didn't know you were so particular about details. But I'll fetch the dress now.'

She left the room and returned almost immediately with a dainty wisp of white satin and green. Poirot took it from her and examined it, handing it back with a bow.

'*Merci, madame*! I see you have had the misfortune to lose one of your green pompons, the one on the shoulder here.'

'Yes, it got torn off at the ball. I picked it up and gave it to poor Lord Cronshaw to keep for me.'

'That was after supper?'

'Yes.'

'Not long before the tragedy, perhaps?'

A faint look of alarm came into Mrs Davidson's pale eyes, and she replied quickly: 'Oh no – long before that. Quite soon after supper, in fact.'

'I see. Well, that is all. I will not derange you further. *Bonjour, madame.*'

'Well,' I said as we emerged from the building, 'that explains the mystery of the green pompon.'

'I wonder.'

'Why, what do you mean?'

'You saw me examine the dress, Hastings?'

'Yes.'

'*Eh bien*, the pompon that was missing had not been wrenched off, as the lady said. On the contrary, it had been *cut* off, my friend, cut off with scissors. The threads were all quite even.'

'Dear me!' I exclaimed. 'This becomes more and more involved.'

'On the contrary,' replied Poirot placidly, 'it becomes more and more simple.'

'Poirot,' I cried, 'one day I shall murder you! Your habit of finding everything perfectly simple is aggravating to the last degree!'

'But when I explain, *mon ami*, is it not always perfectly simple?'

'Yes; that is the annoying part of it! I feel then that I could have done it myself.'

'And so you could, Hastings, so you could. If you would but take the trouble of arranging your ideas! Without method –'

'Yes, yes,' I said hastily, for I knew Poirot's eloquence when started on his favourite theme only too well. 'Tell me, what do we do next? Are you really going to reconstruct the crime?'

'Hardly that. Shall we say that the drama is over, but that I propose to add a – harlequinade?'

IV

The following Tuesday was fixed upon by Poirot as the day for this mysterious performance. The preparations greatly intrigued me. A white screen was erected at one side of the room, flanked by heavy curtains at either side. A man with some lighting apparatus arrived next, and finally a group of members of the theatrical profession, who disappeared into Poirot's bedroom, which had been rigged up as a temporary dressing-room.

Shortly before eight, Japp arrived, in no very cheerful mood. I gathered that the official detective hardly approved of Poirot's plan.

'Bit melodramatic, like all his ideas. But there, it can do no harm, and as he says, it might save us a good bit of trouble. He's been very smart over the case. I was on the same scent myself, of course –' I felt instinctively that Japp was straining the truth here – 'but there, I promised to let him play the thing out his own way. Ah! Here is the crowd.'

His Lordship arrived first, escorting Mrs Mallaby, whom I had not as yet seen. She was a pretty, dark-haired woman, and appeared perceptibly nervous. The Davidsons followed. Chris Davidson also I saw for the first time. He was handsome enough in a rather obvious style, tall and dark, with the easy grace of the actor.

Poirot had arranged seats for the party facing the screen. This was illuminated by a bright light. Poirot switched out the other lights so that the room was in darkness except for the screen. Poirot's voice rose out of the gloom.

'Messieurs, mesdames, a word of explanation. Six figures in turn will pass across the screen. They are familiar to you. Pierrot and his Pierrette; Punchinello the buffoon, and elegant Pulcinella; beautiful Columbine, lightly dancing, Harlequin, the sprite, invisible to man!'

With these words of introduction, the show began. In turn each figure that Poirot had mentioned bounded before the screen, stayed there a moment poised, and then vanished. The lights went up, and a sigh of relief went round. Everyone had been nervous, fearing they knew not what. It seemed to me that the proceedings had gone singularly flat. If the criminal was among us, and Poirot expected him to break down at the mere sight of a familiar figure the device had failed signally – as it was almost bound to do. Poirot, however, appeared not a whit discomposed. He stepped forward, beaming.

'Now, messieurs and mesdames, will you be so good as to tell me, one at a time, what it is that we have just seen? Will you begin, milor'?'

The gentleman looked rather puzzled. 'I'm afraid I don't quite understand.'

'Just tell me what we have been seeing.'

'I – er – well, I should say we have seen six figures passing in front of a screen and dressed to represent the personages in the old Italian Comedy, or – er – ourselves the other night.'

'Never mind the other night, milor',' broke in Poirot. 'The first part of your speech was what I wanted. Madame, you agree with Milor' Cronshaw?'

He had turned as he spoke to Mrs Mallaby.

'I – er – yes, of course.'

'You agree that you have seen six figures representing the Italian Comedy?'

'Why, certainly.'

'Monsieur Davidson? You too?'

'Yes.'

'Madame?'

'Yes.'

'Hastings? Japp? Yes? You are all in accord?'

He looked around upon us; his face grew rather pale, and his eyes were green as any cat's.

'And yet – *you are all wrong*! Your eyes have lied to you – as they lied to you on the night of the Victory Ball. To "see" things with your eyes, as they say, is not always to see the truth. One must see with the eyes of the mind; one must employ the little cells of grey! Know, then, that tonight and on the night of the Victory Ball, you saw not *six* figures but *five*! See!'

The lights went out again. A figure bounded in front of the screen – Pierrot!

'Who is that?' demanded Poirot. 'Is it Pierrot?'

'Yes,' we all cried.

'Look again!'

With a swift movement the man divested himself of his loose Pierrot garb. There in the limelight stood glittering Harlequin! At the same moment there was a cry and an over-turned chair.

'Curse you,' snarled Davidson's voice. 'Curse you! How did you guess?'

Then came the clink of handcuffs and Japp's calm official voice. 'I arrest you, Christopher Davidson – charge of murdering Viscount Cronshaw – anything you say may be used in evidence against you.'

V

It was a quarter of an hour later. A recherché little supper had appeared; and Poirot, beaming all over his face, was dispensing hospitality and answering our eager questions.

'It was all very simple. The circumstances in which the green pompon was found suggested at once that it had been torn from the costume of the murderer. I dismissed Pierrette from my mind (since it takes considerable strength to drive a table-knife home) and fixed upon Pierrot as the criminal. But Pierrot left the ball nearly two hours before the murder was committed. So he must either have returned to the ball later to kill Lord Cronshaw, or – *eh bien*, he must have killed him before he left! Was that impossible? Who had seen Lord Cronshaw after supper that evening? Only Mrs Davidson, whose statement, I suspected, was a deliberate fabrication uttered with the object of accounting for the missing pompon, which, of course, she cut from her own dress to replace the one missing on her husband's costume. But then, Harlequin, who was seen in the box at one-thirty, must have been an impersonation. For a moment, earlier, I had considered the possibility of Mr Beltane being the guilty party. But with his elaborate costume, it was clearly impossible that he could have doubled the roles of Punchinello and Harlequin. On the other hand, to Davidson, a young man of about the same height as the murdered man and an actor by profession, the thing was simplicity itself.

'But one thing worried me. Surely a doctor could not fail to perceive the difference between a man who had been dead two hours and one who had been dead ten minutes! *Eh bien*, the doctor *did* perceive it! But he was not taken to the body and asked, 'How long has this man been dead?' On the contrary, he was informed that the man had been seen alive ten minutes ago, and so he merely commented at the inquest on the abnormal stiffening of the limbs for which he was quite unable to account!

'All was now marching famously for my theory. Davidson had killed Lord Cronshaw immediately after supper, when, as you remember, he was seen to draw him back into the supper–room. Then he departed with Miss Courtenay, left her at the door of her flat (instead of going in and trying to pacify her as he affirmed) and returned post-haste to the Colossus – but as Harlequin, not Pierrot – a simple transformation effected by removing his outer costume.'

VI

The uncle of the dead man leaned forward, his eyes perplexed.

'But if so, he must have come to the ball prepared to kill his victim. What earthly motive could he have had? The motive, that's what I can't get.'

'Ah! There we come to the second tragedy – that of Miss Courtenay. There was one simple point which everyone over-looked. Miss Courtenay died of cocaine poisoning – but her supply of the drug was in the enamel box which was found on Lord Cronshaw's body. Where, then, did she obtain the dose which killed her? Only one person could have supplied her with it – Davidson. And that explains everything. It accounts for her friendship with the Davidsons and her demand that Davidson should escort her home. Lord Cronshaw, who was almost fanati-cally opposed to drug-taking, discovered that she was addicted to cocaine, and suspected that Davidson supplied her with it. Davidson doubtless denied this, but Lord Cronshaw determined to get the truth from Miss Courtenay at the ball. He could forgive the wretched girl, but he would certainly have no mercy on the man who made a living by trafficking in drugs. Exposure and ruin confronted Davidson. He went to the ball determined that Cronshaw's silence must be obtained at any cost.'

'Was Coco's death an accident, then?'

'I suspect that it was an accident cleverly engineered by Davidson. She was furiously angry with Cronshaw, first for his reproaches, and secondly for taking her cocaine from her. Davidson supplied her with more, and probably suggested her augmenting the dose as a defiance to "old Cronch"!'

'One other thing,' I said. 'The recess and the curtain? How did you know about them?'

'Why, *mon ami*, that was the most simple of all. Waiters had been in and out of that little room, so, obviously, the body could not have been lying where it was found on the floor. There must be some place in the room where it could be hidden. I deduced a curtain and a recess behind it. Davidson dragged the body there, and later, after drawing attention to himself in the box, he dragged it out again before finally leaving the Hall. It was one of his best moves. He is a clever fellow!'

But in Poirot's green eyes I read unmistakably the unspoken remark: 'But not quite so clever as Hercule Poirot!'

The Submarine Plans

I

A note had been brought by special messenger. Poirot read it, and a gleam of excitement and interest came into his eyes as he did so. He dismissed the man with a few curt words and then turned to me.

'Pack a bag with all haste, my friend. We're going down to Sharples.'

I started at the mention of the famous country place of Lord Alloway. Head of the newly formed Ministry of Defence, Lord Alloway was a prominent member of the Cabinet. As Sir Ralph Curtis, head of a great engineering firm, he had made his mark in the House of Commons, and he was now freely spoken of as *the* coming man, and the one most likely to be asked to form a ministry should the rumours as to Mr David MacAdam's health prove well founded.

A big Rolls-Royce car was waiting for us below, and as we glided off into the darkness, I plied Poirot with questions.

'What on earth can they want us for at this time of night?' I demanded. It was past eleven.

Poirot shook his head. 'Something of the most urgent, without doubt.'

'I remember,' I said, 'that some years ago there was some rather ugly scandal about Ralph Curtis, as he then was – some jugglery with shares, I believe. In the end, he was completely exonerated; but perhaps something of the kind has arisen again?'

'It would hardly be necessary for him to send for me in the middle of the night, my friend.'

I was forced to agree, and the remainder of the journey was passed in silence. Once out of London, the powerful car forged rapidly ahead, and we arrived at Sharples in a little under the hour.

A pontifical butler conducted us at once to a small study where Lord Alloway was awaiting us. He sprang up to greet us – a tall, spare man who seemed actually to radiate power and vitality.

'M. Poirot, I am delighted to see you. It is the second time the government has demanded your services. I remember only too well what you did for us during the war, when the Prime Minister was kidnapped in that astounding fashion. Your masterly deductions – and may I add, your discretion? – saved the situation.'

Poirot's eyes twinkled a little.

'Do I gather then, milor', that this is another case for – discretion?'

'Most emphatically. Sir Harry and I – oh, let me intoduce you – Admiral Sir Harry Weardale, our First Sea Lord – M. Poirot and – let me see, Captain –'

'Hastings,' I supplied.

'I've often heard of you, M. Poirot,' said Sir Harry, shaking hands. 'This is a most unaccountable business, and if you can solve it, we'll be extremely grateful to you.'

I liked the First Sea Lord immediately, a square, bluff sailor of the good old-fashioned type.

Poirot looked inquiringly at them both, and Alloway took up the tale.

'Of course, you understand that all this is in confidence, M. Poirot. We have had a most serious loss. The plans of the new Z type of submarine have been stolen.'

'When was that?'

'Tonight – less than three hours ago. You can appreciate perhaps, M. Poirot, the magnitude of the disaster. It is essential that the loss should not be made public. I will give you the facts as briefly as possible. My guests over the week-end were the Admiral, here, his wife and son, and Mrs Conrad, a lady well known in London society. The ladies retired to bed early – about ten o'clock; so did Mr Leonard Weardale. Sir Harry is down here partly for the purpose of discussing the construction of this new type of submarine with me. Accordingly, I asked Mr Fitzroy, my secretary, to get out the plans from the safe in the corner there, and to arrange them ready for me, as well as various other documents that bore upon the subject in hand. While he was doing this, the Admiral and I strolled up and down the terrace, smoking cigars and enjoying the warm June air. We finished our smoke and our chat, and decided to get down to business. Just as we turned at the far end of the terrace, I fancied I saw a shadow slip out of the french window here, cross the terrace, and disappear. I paid very little attention, however. I knew Fitzroy to be in this room, and it never entered my head that anything might be amiss. There, of course, I am to blame. Well, we retraced our steps along the terrace and entered this room by the window just as Fitzroy entered it from the hall.

'"Got everything out we are likely to need, Fitzroy?" I asked.

'"I think so, Lord Alloway. The papers are all on your desk," he answered. And then he wished us both good night.

'"Just wait a minute," I said, going to the desk. "I may want something I haven't mentioned."

'I looked quickly through the papers that were lying there.

'"You've forgotten the most important of the lot, Fitzroy," I said. "The actual plans of the submarine!"

'"The plans are right on top, Lord Alloway."

'"Oh no, they're not," I said, turning over the papers.

'"But I put them there not a minute ago!"

'"Well, they're not here now," I said.

'Fitzroy advanced with a bewildered expression on his face. The thing seemed incredible. We turned over the papers on the desk; we hunted through the safe; but at last we had to make up our minds to it that the papers were gone – and gone within the short space of about three minutes while Fitzroy was absent from the room.'

'Why did he leave the room?' asked Poirot quickly.

'Just what I asked him,' exclaimed Sir Harry.

'It appears,' said Lord Alloway, 'that just when he had finished arranging the papers on my desk, he was startled by hearing a woman scream. He dashed out into the hall. On the stairs he discovered Mrs Conrad's French maid. The girl looked very white and upset, and declared that she had seen a ghost – a tall figure dressed all in white that moved without a sound. Fitzroy laughed at her fears and told her, in more or less polite language, not to be a fool. Then he returned to this room just as we entered from the window.'

'It all seems very clear,' said Poirot thoughtfully. 'The only question is, was the maid an accomplice? Did she scream by arrangement with her confederate lurking outside, or was he merely waiting there in the hope of an opportunity presenting itself? It was a man, I suppose – not a woman you saw?'

'I can't tell you, M. Poirot. It was just a – shadow.'

The admiral gave such a peculiar snort that it could not fail to attract attention.

'M. l'Amiral has something to say, I think,' said Poirot quietly, with a slight smile. 'You saw this shadow, Sir Harry?'

'No, I didn't,' returned the other. 'And neither did Alloway. The branch of a tree flapped, or something, and then afterwards, when we discovered the theft, he leaped to the conclusion that he had seen someone pass across the terrace. His imagination played a trick on him; that's all.'

'I am not usually credited with having much imagination,' said Lord Alloway with a slight smile.

'Nonsense, we've all got imagination. We can all work ourselves up to believe that we've seen more than we have. I've had a lifetime of experience at sea, and I'll back my eyes against those of any landsman. I was looking right down the terrace, and I'd have seen the same if there was anything to see.'

He was quite excited over the matter. Poirot rose and stepped quickly to the window.

'You permit?' he asked. 'We must settle this point if possible.'

He went out upon the terrace, and we followed him. He had taken an electric torch from his pocket, and was playing the light along the edge of the grass that bordered the terrace.

'Where did he cross the terrace, milor'?' he asked.

'About opposite the window, I should say.'

Poirot continued to play the torch for some minutes longer, walking the entire length of the terrace and back. Then he shut it off and straightened himself up.

'Sir Harry is right – and you are wrong, milor', he said quietly. 'It rained heavily earlier this evening. Anyone who passed over that grass could not avoid leaving footmarks. But there are none – none at all.'

His eyes went from one man's face to the other's. Lord Alloway looked bewildered and unconvinced; the Admiral expressed a noisy gratification.

'Knew I couldn't be wrong,' he declared. 'Trust my eyes anywhere.'

He was such a picture of an honest old sea-dog that I could not help smiling.

'So that brings us to the people in the house,' said Poirot smoothly. 'Let us come inside again. Now, milor', while Mr Fitzroy was speaking to the maid on the stairs, could anyone have seized the opportunity to enter the study from the hall?'

Lord Alloway shook his head.

'Quite impossible – they would have had to pass him in order to do so.'

'And Mr Fitzroy himself – you are sure of him, eh?'

Lord Alloway flushed.

'Absolutely, M. Poirot. I will answer confidently for my secretary. It is quite impossible that he should be concerned in the matter in any way.'

'Everything seems to be impossible,' remarked Poirot rather drily. 'Possibly the plans attached to themselves a little pair of wings, and flew away – *comme ça*!' He blew his lips out like a comical cherub.

'The whole thing is impossible,' declared Lord Alloway impatiently. 'But I beg, M. Poirot, that you will not dream of suspecting Fitzroy. Consider for one moment – had he wished to take the plans, what could have been easier for him than to take a tracing of them without going to the trouble of stealing them?'

'There, milor',' said Poirot with approval, 'you make a remark *bien juste* – I see that you have a mind orderly and methodical. *L'Angleterre* is happy in possessing you.'

Lord Alloway looked rather embarrassed by this sudden burst of praise. Poirot returned to the matter in hand.

'The room in which you had been sitting all the evening –'

'The drawing-room? Yes?'

'That also has a window on the terrace, since I remember your saying you went out that way. Would it not be possible for someone to come out by the drawing-room window and in by this one while Mr Fitzroy was out of the room, and return the same way?'

'But we'd have seen them,' objected the Admiral.

'Not if you had your backs turned, walking the other way.'

'Fitzroy was only out of the room a few minutes, the time it would take us to walk to the end and back.'

'No matter – it is a possibility – in fact, the only one as things stand.'

'But there was no one in the drawing-room when we went out,' said the Admiral.

'They may have come there afterwards.'

'You mean,' said Lord Alloway slowly, 'that when Fitzroy heard the maid scream and went out, someone was already concealed in the drawing-room, and that they darted in and out through the windows, and only left the drawing-room when Fitzroy had returned to this room?'

'The methodical mind again,' said Poirot, bowing. 'You express the matter perfectly.'

'One of the servants, perhaps?'

'Or a guest. It was Mrs Conrad's maid who screamed. What exactly can you tell me of Mrs Conrad?'

Lord Alloway considered for a minute.

'I told you that she is a lady well known in society. That is true in the sense that she gives large parties, and goes everywhere. But very little is known as to where she really comes from, and what her past life has been. She is a lady who frequents diplomatic and Foreign Office circles as much as possible. The Secret Service is inclined to ask – why?'

'I see,' said Poirot. 'And she was asked here this week-end –'

'So that – shall we say? – we might observe her at close quarters.'

'*Parfaitement*! It is possible that she has turned the tables on you rather neatly.'

Lord Alloway looked discomfited, and Poirot continued: 'Tell me, milor', was any reference made in her hearing to the subjects you and the Admiral were going to discuss together?'

'Yes,' admitted the other. 'Sir Harry said: "And now for our submarine! To work!" or something of that sort. The others had left the room, but she had come back for a book.'

'I see,' said Poirot thoughtfully. 'Milor', it is very late – but this is an urgent affair. I would like to question the members of this house-party at once if it is possible.'

'It can be managed, of course,' said Lord Alloway. 'The awkward thing is, we don't want to let it get about more than can be helped. Of course, Lady Juliet Weardale and young Leonard are all right – but Mrs Conrad, if she is not guilty, is rather a different proposition. Perhaps you could just state that an important paper is missing, without specifying what it is, or going into any of the circumstances of the disappearance?'

'Exactly what I was about to propose myself,' said Poirot, beaming. 'In fact, in all three cases. Monsieur the Admiral will pardon me, but even the best of wives –'

'No offence,' said Sir Harry. 'All women talk, bless 'em! I wish Juliet would talk a little more and play bridge a little less. But women are like that nowadays, never happy unless they're dancing or gambling. I'll get Juliet and Leonard up, shall I, Alloway?'

'Thank you. I'll call the French maid. M. Poirot will want to see her, and she can rouse her mistress. I'll attend to it now. In the meantime, I'll send Fitzroy along.'

II

Mr Fitzroy was a pale, thin young man with pince-nez and a frigid expression. His statement was practically word for word what Lord Alloway had already told us.

'What is your own theory, Mr Fitzroy?'

Mr Fitzroy shrugged his shoulders.

'Undoubtedly someone who knew the hang of things was waiting his chance outside. He could see what went on through the window, and he slipped in when I left the room. It's a pity Lord Alloway didn't give chase then and there when he saw the fellow leave.'

Poirot did not undeceive him. Instead he asked: 'Do you

believe the story of the French maid – that she had seen a ghost?'

'Well, hardly, M. Poirot!'

'I mean – that she really thought so?'

'Oh, as to that, I can't say. She certainly seemed rather upset. She had her hands to her head.'

'Aha!' cried Poirot with the air of one who has made a discovery. 'Is that so indeed – and she was without doubt a pretty girl?'

'I didn't notice particularly,' said Mr Fitzroy in a repressive voice.

'You did not see her mistress, I suppose?'

'As a matter of fact, I did. She was in the gallery at the top of the steps and was calling her – "Léonie!" Then she saw me – and of course retired.'

'Upstairs,' said Poirot, frowning.

'Of course, I realize that all this is very unpleasant for me – or rather would have been, if Lord Alloway had not chanced to see the man actually leaving. In any case, I should be glad if you would make a point of searching my room – and myself.'

'You really wish that?'

'Certainly I do.'

What Poirot would have replied I do not know, but at that moment Lord Alloway reappeared and informed us that the two ladies and Mr Leonard Weardale were in the drawing-room.

The women were in becoming negligees. Mrs Conrad was a beautiful woman of thirty-five, with golden hair and a slight tendency to *embonpoint*. Lady Juliet Weardale must have been forty, tall and dark, very thin, still beautiful, with exquisite hands and feet, and a restless, haggard manner. Her son was rather an effeminate-looking young man, as great a contrast to his bluff, hearty father as could well be imagined.

Poirot gave forth the little rigmarole we had agreed upon,

and then explained that he was anxious to know if anyone had heard or seen anything that night which might assist us.

Turning to Mrs Conrad first, he asked her if she would be so kind as to inform him exactly what her movements had been.

'Let me see . . . I went upstairs. I rang for my maid. Then, as she did not put in an appearance, I came out and called her. I could hear her talking on the stairs. After she had brushed my hair, I sent her away – she was in a very curious nervous state. I read awhile and then went to bed.'

'And you, Lady Juliet?'

'I went straight upstairs and to bed. I was very tired.'

'What about your book, dear?' asked Mrs Conrad with a sweet smile.

'My book?' Lady Juliet flushed.

'Yes, you know, when I sent Léonie away, you were coming up the stairs. You had been down to the drawing-room for a book, you said.'

'Oh yes, I did go down. I – I forgot.'

Lady Juliet clasped her hands nervously together.

'Did you hear Mrs Conrad's maid scream, milady?'

'No – no, I didn't.'

'How curious – because you must have been in the drawing-room at the time.'

'I heard nothing,' said Lady Juliet in a firmer voice.

Poirot turned to young Leonard.

'Monsieur?'

'Nothing doing. I went straight upstairs and turned in.'

Poirot stroked his chin.

'Alas, I fear there is nothing to help me here. Mesdames and monsieur, I regret – I regret infinitely to have deranged you from your slumbers for so little. Accept my apologies, I pray of you.'

Gesticulating and apologizing, he marshalled them out. He

returned with the French maid, a pretty, impudent-looking girl. Alloway and Weardale had gone out with the ladies.

'Now, mademoiselle,' said Poirot in a brisk tone, 'let us have the truth. Recount to me no histories. Why did you scream on the stairs?'

'Ah, monsieur, I saw a tall figure – all in white –'

Poirot arrested her with an energetic shake of his forefinger.

'Did I not say, recount to me no histories? I will make a guess. He kissed you, did he not? M. Leonard Weardale, I mean?'

'*Eh bien, monsieur,* and after all, what is a kiss?'

'Under the circumstances, it is most natural,' replied Poirot gallantly. 'I myself, or Hastings here – but tell me just what occurred.'

'He came up behind me, and caught me. I was startled, and I screamed. If I had known, I would not have screamed – but he came upon me like a cat. Then came *M. le secrétaire.* M. Leonard flew up the stairs. And what could I say? Especially to a *jeune homme comme ça – tellement comme il faut? Ma foi,* I invent a ghost.'

'And all is explained,' cried Poirot genially. 'You then mounted to the chamber of Madame your mistress. Which is her room, by the way?'

'It is at the end, monsieur. That way.'

'Directly over the study, then. *Bien,* mademoiselle, I will detain you no longer. And *la prochaine fois,* do not scream.'

Handing her out, he came back to me with a smile.

'An interesting case, is it not, Hastings? I begin to have a few little ideas. *Et vous?*'

'What was Leonard Weardale doing on the stairs? I don't like that young man, Poirot. He's a thorough young rake, I should say.'

'I agree with you, *mon ami.*'

'Fitzroy seems an honest fellow.'

'Lord Alloway is certainly insistent on that point.'

'And yet there is something in his manner –'

'That is almost too good to be true? I felt it myself. On the other hand, our friend Mrs Conrad is certainly no good at all.'

'And her room is over the study,' I said musingly, and keeping a sharp eye on Poirot.

He shook his head with a slight smile.

'No, *mon ami*, I cannot bring myself seriously to believe that that immaculate lady swarmed down the chimney, or let herself down from the balcony.'

As he spoke, the door opened, and to my great surprise, Lady Juliet Weardale flitted in.

'M. Poirot,' she said somewhat breathlessly, 'Can I speak to you alone?'

'Milady, Captain Hastings is as my other self. You can speak before him as though he were a thing of no account, not there at all. Be seated, I pray you.'

She sat down, still keeping her eyes fixed on Poirot.

'What I have to say is – rather difficult. You are in charge of this case. If the – papers were to be returned, would that end the matter? I mean, could it be done without questions being asked?'

Poirot stared hard at her.

'Let me understand you, madame. They are to be placed in my hand – is that right? And I am to return them to Lord Alloway on the condition that he asks no questions as to where I got them?'

She bowed her head. 'That is what I mean. But I must be sure there will be no – publicity.'

'I do not think Lord Alloway is particularly anxious for publicity,' said Poirot grimly.

'You accept then?' she cried eagerly in response.

'A little moment, milady. It depends on how soon you can place those papers in my hands.'

'Almost immediately.'

Poirot glanced up at the clock.

'How soon, exactly?'

'Say – ten minutes,' she whispered.

'I accept, milady.'

She hurried from the room. I pursed my mouth up for a whistle.

'Can you sum up the situation for me, Hastings?'

'Bridge,' I replied succinctly.

'Ah, you remember the careless words of Monsieur the Admiral! What a memory! I felicitate you, Hastings.'

We said no more, for Lord Alloway came in, and looked inquiringly at Poirot.

'Have you any further ideas, M. Poirot? I am afraid the answers to your questions have been rather disappointing.'

'Not at all, milor'. They have been quite sufficiently illuminating. It will be unnecessary for me to stay here any longer, and so, with your permission, I will return at once to London.'

Lord Alloway seemed dumbfounded.

'But – but what have you discovered? Do you know who took the plans?'

'Yes, milor', I do. Tell me – in the case of the papers being returned to you anonymously, you would prosecute no further inquiry?'

Lord Alloway stared at him.

'Do you mean on payment of a sum of money?'

'No, milor', returned unconditionally.'

'Of course, the recovery of the plans is the great thing,' said Lord Alloway slowly. He looked puzzled and uncomprehending.

'Then I should seriously recommend you to adopt that course. Only you, the Admiral and your secretary know of the loss. Only they need know of the restitution. And you may count on me to support you in every way – lay the mystery on my shoulders. You asked me to restore the papers – I have done so. You know no more.' He rose and held out his hand. 'Milor', I am glad to have met you. I have faith in you – and your devotion to England. You will guide her destinies with a strong, sure hand.'

'M. Poirot – I swear to you that I will do my best. It may be a fault, or it may be a virtue – but I believe in myself.'

'So does every great man. Me, I am the same!' said Poirot grandiloquently.

III

The car came round to the door in a few minutes, and Lord Alloway bade us farewell on the steps with renewed cordiality.

'That is a great man, Hastings,' said Poirot as we drove off. 'He has brains, resource, power. He is the strong man that England needs to guide her through these difficult days of reconstruction.'

'I'm quite ready to agree with all you say, Poirot – but what about Lady Juliet? Is she to return the papers straight to Alloway? What will she think when she finds you have gone off without a word?'

'Hastings, I will ask you a little question. Why, when she was talking with me, did she not hand me the plans then and there?'

'She hadn't got them with her.'

'Perfectly. How long would it take her to fetch them from her room? Or from any hiding-place in the house? You need not answer. I will tell you. Probably about two minutes and a half! Yet she asks for ten minutes. Why? Clearly she has to obtain them from some other person, and to reason or argue with that person before they give them up. Now, what person could that be? Not Mrs Conrad, clearly, but a member of her own family, her husband or son. Which is it likely to be?

Leonard Weardale said he went straight to bed. We know that to be untrue. Supposing his mother went to his room and found it empty; supposing she came down filled with a nameless dread – he is no beauty that son of hers! She does not find him, but later she hears him deny that he ever left his room. She leaps to the conclusion that he is the thief. Hence her interview with me.

'But, *mon ami*, we know something that Lady Juliet does not. We know that her son could not have been in the study, because he was on the stairs, making love to the pretty French maid. Although she does not know it, Leonard Weardale has an alibi.'

'Well, then, who did steal the papers? We seem to have eliminated everybody – Lady Juliet, her son, Mrs Conrad, the French maid –'

'Exactly. Use your little grey cells, my friend. The solution stares you in the face.'

I shook my head blankly.

'But yes! If you would only persevere! See, then, Fitzroy goes out of the study; he leaves the papers on the desk. A few minutes later Lord Alloway enters the room, goes to the desk, and the papers are gone. Only two things are possible: either Fitzroy did *not* leave the papers on the desk, but put them in his pocket – and that is not reasonable, because, as Alloway pointed out, he could have taken a tracing at his own convenience any time – or else the papers were still on the desk when Lord Alloway went to it – in which case they went into his pocket.'

'Lord Alloway the thief,' I said, dumbfounded. 'But why? Why?'

'Did you not tell me of some scandal in the past? He was exonerated, you said. But suppose, after all, it had been true? In English public life there must be no scandal. If this were raked up and proved against him now – goodbye to his political career. We will suppose that he was being black-mailed, and the price asked was the submarine plans.'

'But the man's a black traitor!' I cried.

'Oh no, he is not. He is clever and resourceful. Supposing, my friend, that he copied those plans, making – for he is a clever engineer – a slight alteration in each part which will render them quite impractible. He hands the faked plans to the enemy's agent – Mrs Conrad, I fancy; but in order that no suspicion of their genuineness may arise, the plans must seem to be stolen. He does his best to throw no suspicion on anyone in the house, by pretending to see a man leaving the window. But there he ran up against the obstinacy of the Admiral. So his next anxiety is that no suspicion shall fall on Fitzroy.'

'This is all guesswork on your part, Poirot,' I objected.

'It is psychology, *mon ami*. A man who had handed over the real plans would not be overscrupulous as to who was likely to fall under suspicion. And why was he so anxious that no details of the robbery should be given to Mrs Conrad? Because he had handed over the faked plans earlier in the evening, and did not want her to know that the theft could only have taken place later.'

'I wonder if you are right,' I said.

'Of course I am right. I spoke to Alloway as one great man to another – and he understood perfectly. You will see.'

IV

One thing is quite certain. On the day when Lord Alloway became Prime Minister, a cheque and a signed photograph arrived; on the photograph were the words: '*To my discreet friend, Hercule Poirot – from Alloway.*'

I believe that the Z type of submarine is causing great exultation in naval circles. They say it will revolutionize modern naval warfare. I have heard that a certain foreign power essayed to construct something of the same kind and the result was a dismal failure. But I still consider that Poirot was guessing. He will do it once too often one of these days.

How Does Your Garden Grow?

I

Hercule Poirot arranged his letters in a neat pile in front of him. He picked up the topmost letter, studied the address for a moment, then neatly slit the back of the envelope with a little paper-knife that he kept on the breakfast table for that express purpose and extracted the contents. Inside was yet another envelope, carefully sealed with purple wax and marked 'Private and Confidential'.

Hercule Poirot's eyebrows rose a little on his egg-shaped head. He murmured, '*Patience! Nous allons arriver!*' and once more brought the little paper-knife into play. This time the envelope yielded a letter – written in a rather shaky and spiky handwriting. Several words were heavily underlined.

Hercule Poirot unfolded it and read. The letter was headed once again 'Private and Confidential'. On the right-hand side was the address – Rosebank, Charman's Green, Bucks – and the date – March twenty-first.

Dear M. Poirot,
I have been recommended to you by an old and valued friend of
mine who knows the worry *and* distress *I have been in lately.*
Not that this friend knows the actual circumstances – *those I*
have kept entirely *to myself – the matter being strictly private.*
My friend assures me that you are discretion *itself – and that*
there will be no fear of my being involved in a police *matter*
which, if my suspicions should prove correct, I should very *much*

dislike. *But it is of course possible that I am* entirely *mistaken. I do not feel myself clear-headed enough nowadays – suffering as I do from insomnia and the result of a severe illness last winter – to investigate things for myself. I have neither the* means *nor the* ability. *On the other hand, I must reiterate once more that this is a very delicate family matter and that for many reasons I may want the* whole thing hushed up. *If I am once assured of the* facts, *I can deal with the matter myself and should prefer to do so. I hope that I have made myself clear on this point. If you will undertake this investigation perhaps you will let me know to the above address?*

    Yours very truly,
    Amelia Barrowby

Poirot read the letter through twice. Again his eyebrows rose slightly. Then he placed it on one side and proceeded to the next envelope in the pile.

At ten o'clock precisely he entered the room where Miss Lemon, his confidential secretary, sat awaiting her instructions for the day. Miss Lemon was forty-eight and of unprepossessing appearance. Her general effect was that of a lot of bones flung together at random. She had a passion for order almost equalling that of Poirot himself; and though capable of thinking, she never thought unless told to do so.

Poirot handed her the morning correspondence. 'Have the goodness, mademoiselle, to write refusals couched in correct terms to all of these.'

Miss Lemon ran an eye over the various letters, scribbling in turn a hieroglyphic on each of them. These marks were legible to her alone and were in a code of her own: 'Soft soap'; 'slap in the face'; 'purr purr'; 'curt'; and so on. Having done this, she nodded and looked up for further instructions.

Poirot handed her Amelia Barrowby's letter. She extracted it from its double envelope, read it through and looked up inquiringly.

'Yes, M. Poirot?' Her pencil hovered – ready – over her shorthand pad.

'What is your opinion of that letter, Miss Lemon?'

With a slight frown Miss Lemon put down the pencil and read through the letter again.

The contents of a letter meant nothing to Miss Lemon except from the point of view of composing an adequate reply. Very occasionally her employer appealed to her human, as opposed to her official, capacities. It slightly annoyed Miss Lemon when he did so – she was very nearly the perfect machine, completely and gloriously uninterested in all human affairs. Her real passion in life was the perfection of a filing system beside which all other filing systems should sink into oblivion. She dreamed of such a system at night. Nevertheless, Miss Lemon was perfectly capable of intelligence on purely human matters, as Hercule Poirot well knew.

'Well?' he demanded.

'Old lady,' said Miss Lemon. 'Got the wind up pretty badly.'

'Ah! The wind rises in her, you think?'

Miss Lemon, who considered that Poirot had been long enough in Great Britain to understand its slang terms, did not reply. She took a brief look at the double envelope.

'Very hush-hush,' she said. 'And tells you nothing at all.'

'Yes,' said Hercule Poirot. 'I observed that.'

Miss Lemon's hand hung once more hopefully over the shorthand pad. This time Hercule Poirot responded.

'Tell her I will do myself the honour to call upon her at any time she suggests, unless she prefers to consult me here. Do not type the letter – write it by hand.'

'Yes, M. Poirot.'

Poirot produced more correspondence. 'These are bills.'

Miss Lemon's efficient hands sorted them quickly. 'I'll pay all but these two.'

'Why those two? There is no error in them.'

'They are firms you've only just begun to deal with. It looks bad to pay too promptly when you've just opened an account – looks as though you were working up to get some credit later on.'

'Ah!' murmured Poirot. 'I bow to your superior knowledge of the British tradesman.'

'There's nothing much I don't know about them,' said Miss Lemon grimly.

II

The letter to Miss Amelia Barrowby was duly written and sent, but no reply was forthcoming. Perhaps, thought Hercule Poirot, the old lady had unravelled her mystery herself. Yet he felt a shade of surprise that in that case she should not have written a courteous word to say that his services were no longer required.

It was five days later when Miss Lemon, after receiving her morning's instructions, said, 'That Miss Barrowby we wrote to – no wonder there's been no answer. She's dead.'

Hercule Poirot said very softly, 'Ah – dead.' It sounded not so much like a question as an answer.

Opening her handbag, Miss Lemon produced a newspaper cutting. 'I saw it in the tube and tore it out.'

Just registering in his mind approval of the fact that, though Miss Lemon used the word 'tore', she had neatly cut the entry with scissors, Poirot read the announcement taken from the Births, Deaths and Marriages in the *Morning Post*: 'On March 26th – suddenly – at Rosebank, Charman's Green, Amelia Jan Barrowby, in her seventy-third year. No flowers, by request.'

Poirot read it over. He murmured under his breath, 'Suddenly.' Then he said briskly, 'If you will be so obliging as to take a letter, Miss Lemon?'

The pencil hovered. Miss Lemon, her mind dwelling on the intricacies of the filing system, took down in rapid and correct shorthand:

Dear Miss Barrowby,
I have received no reply from you, but as I shall be in the neighbourhood of Charman's Green on Friday, I will call upon you on that day and discuss more fully the matter mentioned to me in your letter.
  Yours, etc.

'Type this letter, please; and if it is posted at once, it should get to Charman's Green tonight.'

On the following morning a letter in a black-edged envelope arrived by the second post:

Dear Sir,
In reply to your letter my aunt, Miss Barrowby, passed away on the twenty-sixth, so the matter you speak of is no longer of importance.
  Yours truly,
  Mary Delafontaine

Poirot smiled to himself. 'No longer of importance . . . Ah – that is what we shall see. *En avant* – to Charman's Green.'

Rosebank was a house that seemed likely to live up to its name, which is more than can be said for most houses of its class and character.

Hercule Poirot paused as he walked up the path to the front door and looked approvingly at the neatly planned beds on either side of him. Rose trees that promised a good harvest later in the year, and at present daffodils, early tulips, blue hyacinths – the last bed was partly edged with shells.

Poirot murmured to himself, 'How does it go, the English rhyme the children sing?

'Mistress Mary, quite contrary,
How does your garden grow?
With cockle-shells, and silver bells.
And pretty maids all in a row.

'Not a row, perhaps,' he considered, 'but here is at least one pretty maid to make the little rhyme come right.'

The front door had opened and a neat little maid in cap and apron was looking somewhat dubiously at the spectacle of a heavily moustached foreign gentleman talking aloud to himself in the front garden. She was, as Poirot had noted, a very pretty little maid, with round blue eyes and rosy cheeks.

Poirot raised his hat with courtesy and addressed her: 'Pardon, but does a Miss Amelia Barrowby live here?'

The little maid gasped and her eyes grew rounder. 'Oh, sir, didn't you know? She's dead. Ever so sudden it was. Tuesday night.'

She hesitated, divided between two strong instincts: the first, distrust of a foreigner; the second, the pleasurable enjoyment of her class in dwelling on the subject of illness and death.

'You amaze me,' said Hercule Poirot, not very truthfully. 'I had an appointment with the lady for today. However, I can perhaps see the other lady who lives here.'

The little maid seemed slightly doubtful. 'The mistress? Well, you could see her, perhaps, but I don't know whether she'll be seeing anyone or not.'

'She will see me,' said Poirot, and handed her a card.

The authority of his tone had its effect. The rosy-cheeked maid fell back and ushered Poirot into a sitting-room on the right of the hall. Then, card in hand, she departed to summon her mistress.

Hercule Poirot looked round him. The room was a perfectly conventional drawing-room – oatmeal-coloured paper with a frieze round the top, indeterminate cretonnes, rose-coloured cushions and curtains, a good many china knick-knacks and ornaments. There was nothing in the room that stood out, that announced a definite personality.

Suddenly Poirot, who was very sensitive, felt eyes watching him. He wheeled round. A girl was standing in the entrance of the french window – a small, sallow girl, with very black hair and suspicious eyes.

She came in, and as Poirot made a little bow she burst out abruptly, 'Why have you come?'

Poirot did not reply. He merely raised his eyebrows.

'You are not a lawyer – no?' Her English was good, but not for a minute would anyone have taken her to be English.

'Why should I be a lawyer, mademoiselle?'

The girl stared at him sullenly. 'I thought you might be. I thought you had come perhaps to say that she did not know what she was doing. I have heard of such things – the not due influence; that is what they call it, no? But that is not right. She wanted me to have the money, and I shall have it. If it is needful I shall have a lawyer of my own. The money is mine. She wrote it down so, and so it shall be.' She looked ugly, her chin thrust out, her eyes gleaming.

The door opened and a tall woman entered and said, 'Katrina.'

The girl shrank, flushed, muttered something and went out through the window.

Poirot turned to face the newcomer who had so effectually dealt with the situation by uttering a single word. There had been authority in her voice, and contempt and a shade of well-bred irony. He realized at once that this was the owner of the house, Mary Delafontaine.

'M. Poirot? I wrote to you. You cannot have received my letter.'

'Alas, I have been away from London.'

'Oh, I see; that explains it. I must introduce myself. My name is Delafontaine. This is my husband. Miss Barrowby was my aunt.'

Mr Delafontaine had entered so quietly that his arrival had passed unnoticed. He was a tall man with grizzled hair and an indeterminate manner. He had a nervous way of fingering his chin. He looked often towards his wife, and it was plain that he expected her to take the lead in any conversation.

'I must regret that I intrude in the midst of your bereavement,' said Hercule Poirot.

'I quite realize that it is not your fault,' said Mrs Delafontaine. 'My aunt died on Tuesday evening. It was quite unexpected.'

'Most unexpected,' said Mr Delafontaine. 'Great blow.' His eyes watched the window where the foreign girl had disappeared.

'I apologize,' said Hercule Poirot. 'And I withdraw.' He moved a step towards the door.

'Half a sec,' said Mr Delafontaine. 'You – er – had an appointment with Aunt Amelia, you say?'

'*Parfaitement.*'

'Perhaps you will tell us about it,' said his wife. 'If there is anything we can do –'

'It was of a private nature,' said Poirot. 'I am a detective,' he added simply.

Mr Delafontaine knocked over a little china figure he was handling. His wife looked puzzled.

'A detective? And you had an appointment with Auntie? But how extraordinary!' She stared at him. 'Can't you tell us a little more, M. Poirot? It – it seems quite fantastic.'

Poirot was silent for a moment. He chose his words with care.

'It is difficult for me, madame, to know what to do.'

'Look here,' said Mr Delafontaine. 'She didn't mention Russians, did she?'

'Russians?'

'Yes, you know – Bolshies, Reds, all that sort of thing.'

'Don't be absurd, Henry,' said his wife.

Mr Delafontaine collapsed. 'Sorry – sorry – I just wondered.'

Mary Delafontaine looked frankly at Poirot. Her eyes were very blue – the colour of forget-me-nots. 'If you can tell us anything, M. Poirot, I should be glad if you would do so. I can assure you that I have a – a reason for asking.'

Mr Delafontaine looked alarmed. 'Be careful, old girl – you know there may be nothing in it.'

Again his wife quelled him with a glance. 'Well, M. Poirot?'

Slowly, gravely, Hercule Poirot shook his head. He shook it with visible regret, but he shook it. 'At present, madame,' he said, 'I fear I must say nothing.'

He bowed, picked up his hat and moved to the door. Mary Delafontaine came with him into the hall. On the doorstep he paused and looked at her.

'You are fond of your garden, I think, madame?'

'I? Yes, I spend a lot of time gardening.'

Je vous fais mes compliments.

He bowed once more and strode down to the gate. As he passed out of it and turned to the right he glanced back and registered two impressions – a sallow face watching him from the first-floor window, and a man of erect and soldierly carriage pacing up and down on the opposite side of the street.

Hercule Poirot nodded to himself. '*Definitivement*,' he said. 'There is a mouse in this hole! What move must the cat make now?'

His decision took him to the nearest post office. Here he put through a couple of telephone calls. The result seemed to be satisfactory. He bent his steps to Charman's Green police station, where he inquired for Inspector Sims.

Inspector Sims was a big, burly man with a hearty manner. 'M. Poirot?' he inquired. 'I thought so. I've just this minute had a telephone call through from the chief constable about you. He said you'd be dropping in. Come into my office.'

The door shut, the inspector waved Poirot to one chair, settled himself in another, and turned a gaze of acute inquiry upon his visitor.

'You're very quick on to the mark, M. Poirot. Come to see us about this Rosebank case almost before we know it is a case. What put you on to it?'

Poirot drew out the letter he had received and handed it to the inspector. The latter read it with some interest.

'Interesting,' he said. 'The trouble is, it might mean so many things. Pity she couldn't have been a little more explicit. It would have helped us now.'

'Or there might have been no need for help.'

'You mean?'

'She might have been alive.'

'You go as far as that, do you? H'm – I'm not sure you're wrong.'

'I pray of you, Inspector, recount to me the facts. I know nothing at all.'

'That's easily done. Old lady was taken bad after dinner on Tuesday night. Very alarming. Convulsions – spasms – whatnot. They sent for the doctor. By the time he arrived she was dead. Idea was she'd died of a fit. Well, he didn't much like the look of things. He hemmed and hawed and put it with a bit of soft sawder, but he made it clear that he couldn't give a death certificate. And as far as the family go, that's where the matter stands. They're awaiting the result of the post-mortem. We've got a bit further. The doctor gave us the tip right away – he and the police surgeon did the autopsy together – and the result is in no doubt whatever. The old lady died of a large dose of strychnine.'

'Aha!'

'That's right. Very nasty bit of work. Point is, who gave it to her? It must have been administered very shortly before death. First idea was it was given to her in her food at dinner – but, frankly, that seems to be a washout. They had artichoke soup, served from a tureen, fish pie and apple tart.

'Miss Barrowby, Mr Delafontaine and Mrs Delafontaine. Miss Barrowby had a kind of nurse-attendant – a half-Russian girl – but she didn't eat with the family. She had the remains as they came out from the dining-room. There's a maid, but it was her night out. She left the soup on the stove and the fish pie in the oven, and the apple tart was cold. All three of them ate the same thing – and, apart from that, I don't think you could get strychnine down anyone's throat that way. Stuff's as bitter as gall. The doctor told me you could taste it in a solution of one in a thousand, or something like that.'

'Coffee?'

'Coffee's more like it, but the old lady never took coffee.'

'I see your point. Yes, it seems an insuperable difficulty. What did she drink at the meal?'

'Water.'

'Worse and worse.'

'Bit of a teaser, isn't it?'

'She had money, the old lady?'

'Very well to do, I imagine. Of course, we haven't got exact details yet. The Delafontaines are pretty badly off, from what I can make out. The old lady helped with the upkeep of the house.'

Poirot smiled a little. He said, 'So you suspect the Delafontaines. Which of them?'

'I don't exactly say I suspect either of them in particular. But there it is; they're her only near relations, and her death brings them a tidy sum of money, I've no doubt. We all know what human nature is!'

'Sometimes inhuman – yes, that is very true. And there was nothing else the old lady ate or drank?'

'Well, as a matter of fact –'

'Ah, *voilà*! I felt that you had something, as you say, up your sleeve – the soup, the fish pie, the apple tart – a *bêtise*! Now we come to the hub of the affair.'

'I don't know about that. But as a matter of fact, the old girl took a cachet before meals. You know, not a pill or a tablet; one of those rice-paper things with a powder inside. Some perfectly harmless thing for the digestion.'

'Admirable. Nothing is easier than to fill a cachet with strychnine and substitute it for one of the others. It slips down the throat with a drink of water and is not tasted.'

'That's all right. The trouble is, the girl gave it to her.'

'The Russian girl?'

'Yes. Katrina Rieger. She was a kind of lady-help, nurse-companion to Miss Barrowby. Fairly ordered about by her, too, I gather. Fetch this, fetch that, fetch the other, rub my back, pour out my medicine, run round to the chemist – all that sort of business. You know how it is with these old women – they mean to be kind, but what they need is a sort of black slave!'

Poirot smiled.

'And there you are, you see,' continued Inspector Sims. 'It doesn't fit in what you might call nicely. Why should the girl poison her? Miss Barrowby dies and now the girl will be out of a job, and jobs aren't easy to find – she's not trained or anything.'

'Still,' suggested Poirot, 'if the box of cachets was left about, anyone in the house might have the opportunity.'

'Naturally we're making inquiries – quiet like, if you understand me. When the prescription was last made up, where it was usually kept; patience and a lot of spade work – that's what will do the trick in the end. And then there's Miss Barrowby's solicitor. I'm having an interview with him tomorrow. And the bank manager. There's a lot to be done still.'

Poirot rose. 'A little favour, Inspector Sims; you will send me a little word how the affair marches. I would esteem it a great favour. Here is my telephone number.'

'Why, certainly, M. Poirot. Two heads are better than one; and besides, you ought to be in on this, having had that letter and all.'

'You are too amiable, Inspector.' Politely, Poirot shook hands and took his leave.

III

He was called to the telephone on the following afternoon. 'Is that M. Poirot? Inspector Sims here. Things are beginning to sit up and look pretty in the little matter you and I know of.'

'In verity? Tell me, I pray of you.'

'Well, here's item No. I – and a pretty big item. Miss B. left a small legacy to her niece and everything else to K. In consideration of her great kindness and attention – that's the way it was put. That alters the complexion of things.'

A picture rose swiftly in Poirot's mind. A sullen face and a passionate voice saying, 'The money is mine. She wrote it down and so it shall be.' The legacy would not come as a surprise to Katrina – she knew about it beforehand.

'Item No. 2,' continued the voice of Inspector Sims. 'Nobody but K. handled that cachet.'

'You can be sure of that?'

'The girl herself doesn't deny it. What do you think of that?'

'Extremely interesting.'

'We only want one thing more – evidence of how the strychnine came into her possession. That oughtn't to be difficult.'

'But so far you haven't been successful?'

'I've barely started. The inquest was only this morning.'

'What happened at it?'

'Adjourned for a week.'

'And the young lady – K.?'

'I'm detaining her on suspicion. Don't want to run any risks. She might have some funny friends in the country who'd try to get her out of it.'

'No,' said Poirot. 'I do not think she has any friends.'

'Really? What makes you say that, M. Poirot?'

'It is just an idea of mine. There were no other "items", as you call them?'

'Nothing that's strictly relevant. Miss B. seems to have been monkeying about a bit with her shares lately – must have dropped quite a tidy sum. It's rather a funny business, one way and another, but I don't see how it affects the main issue – not at present, that is.'

'No, perhaps you are right. Well, my best thanks to you. It was most amiable of you to ring me up.'

'Not at all. I'm a man of my word. I could see you were interested. Who knows, you may be able to give me a helping hand before the end.'

'That would give me great pleasure. It might help you, for instance, if I could lay my hand on a friend of the girl Katrina.'

'I thought you said she hadn't got any friends?' said Inspector Sims, surprised.

'I was wrong,' said Hercule Poirot. 'She has one.'

Before the inspector could ask a further question, Poirot had rung off.

With a serious face he wandered into the room where Miss Lemon sat at her typewriter. She raised her hands from the keys at her employer's approach and looked at him inquiringly.

'I want you,' said Poirot, 'to figure to yourself a little history.'

Miss Lemon dropped her hands into her lap in a resigned

manner. She enjoyed typing, paying bills, filing papers and entering up engagements. To be asked to imagine herself in hypothetical situations bored her very much, but she accepted it as a disagreeable part of a duty.

'You are a Russian girl,' began Poirot.

'Yes,' said Miss Lemon, looking intensely British.

'You are alone and friendless in this country. You have reasons for not wishing to return to Russia. You are employed as a kind of drudge, nurse-attendant and companion to an old lady. You are meek and uncomplaining.'

'Yes,' said Miss Lemon obediently, but entirely failing to see herself being meek to any old lady under the sun.

'The old lady takes a fancy to you. She decides to leave her money to you. She tells you so.' Poirot paused.

Miss Lemon said 'Yes' again.

'And then the old lady finds out something; perhaps it is a matter of money – she may find that you have not been honest with her. Or it might be more grave still – a medicine that tasted different, some food that disagreed. Anyway, she begins to suspect you of something and she writes to a very famous detective – *enfin*, to the most famous detective – me! I am to call upon her shortly. And then, as you say, the dripping will be in the fire. The great thing is to act quickly. And so – before the great detective arrives – the old lady is dead. And the money comes to you . . . Tell me, does that seem to you reasonable?'

'Quite reasonable,' said Miss Lemon. 'Quite reasonable for a Russian, that is. Personally, I should never take a post as a companion. I like my duties clearly defined. And of course I should not dream of murdering anyone.'

Poirot sighed. 'How I miss my friend Hastings. He had such imagination. Such a romantic mind! It is true that he always imagined wrong – but that in itself was a guide.'

Miss Lemon was silent. She looked longingly at the type-written sheet in front of her.

'So it seems to you reasonable,' mused Poirot.

'Doesn't it to you?'

'I am almost afraid it does,' sighed Poirot.

The telephone rang and Miss Lemon went out of the room to answer it. She came back to say 'It's Inspector Sims again.' Poirot hurried to the instrument. ''Allo, 'allo. What is that you say?'

Sims repeated his statement. 'We've found a packet of strychnine in the girl's bedroom – tucked underneath the mattress. The sergeant's just come in with the news. That about clinches it, I think.'

'Yes,' said Poirot, 'I think that clinches it.' His voice had changed. It rang with sudden confidence.

When he had rung off, he sat down at his writing table and arranged the objects on it in a mechanical manner. He murmured to himself, 'There was something wrong. I felt it – no, not felt. It must have been something I saw. *En avant*, the little grey cells. Ponder – reflect. Was everything logical and in order? The girl – her anxiety about the money: Mme Delafontaine; her husband – his suggestion of Russians – imbecile, but he is an imbecile; the room; the garden – ah! Yes, the garden.'

He sat up very stiff. The green light shone in his eyes. He sprang up and went into the adjoining room.

'Miss Lemon, will you have the kindness to leave what you are doing and make an investigation for me?'

'An investigation, M. Poirot? I'm afraid I'm not very good –'

Poirot interrupted her. 'You said one day that you knew all about tradesmen.'

'Certainly I do,' said Miss Lemon with confidence.

'Then the matter is simple. You are to go to Charman's Green and you are to discover a fishmonger.'

'A fishmonger?' asked Miss Lemon, surprised.

'Precisely. The fishmonger who supplied Rosebank with

fish. When you have found him you will ask him a certain question.'

He handed her a slip of paper. Miss Lemon took it, noted its contents without interest, then nodded and slipped the lid on her typewriter.

'We will go to Charman's Green together,' said Poirot. 'You go to the fishmonger and I to the police station. It will take us but half an hour from Baker Street.'

On arrival at his destination, he was greeted by the surprised Inspector Sims. 'Well, this is quick work, M. Poirot. I was talking to you on the phone only an hour ago.'

'I have a request to make to you; that you allow me to see this girl Katrina – what is her name?'

'Katrina Rieger. Well, I don't suppose there's any objection to that.'

The girl Katrina looked even more sallow and sullen than ever.

Poirot spoke to her very gently. 'Mademoiselle, I want you to believe that I am not your enemy. I want you to tell me the truth.'

Her eyes snapped defiantly. 'I have told the truth. To everyone I have told the truth! If the old lady was poisoned, it was not I who poisoned her. It is all a mistake. You wish to prevent me having the money.' Her voice was rasping. She looked, he thought, like a miserable little cornered rat.

'Did no one handle it but you?'

'I have said so, have I not? They were made up at the chemist's that afternoon. I brought them back with me in my bag – that was just before supper. I opened the box and gave Miss Barrowby one with a glass of water.'

'No one touched them but you?'

'No.' A cornered rat – with courage!

'And Miss Barrowby had for supper only what we have been told. The soup, the fish pie, the tart?'

'Yes.' A hopeless 'yes' – dark, smouldering eyes that saw no light anywhere.

Poirot patted her shoulder. 'Be of good courage, mademoiselle. There may yet be freedom – yes, and money – a life of ease.'

She looked at him suspiciously.

As she went out Sims said to him, 'I didn't quite get what you said through the telephone – something about the girl having a friend.'

'She has one. Me!' said Hercule Poirot, and had left the police station before the inspector could pull his wits together.

IV

At the Green Cat tearooms, Miss Lemon did not keep her employer waiting. She went straight to the point.

'The man's name is Rudge, in the High Street, and you were quite right. A dozen and a half exactly. I've made a note of what he said.' She handed it to him.

'Arrr.' It was a deep, rich sound like a purr of a cat.

V

Hercule Poirot betook himself to Rosebank. As he stood in the front garden, the sun setting behind him, Mary Delafontaine came out to him.

'M. Poirot?' Her voice sounded surprised. 'You have come back?'

'Yes, I have come back.' He paused and then said, 'When I first came here, madame, the children's nursery rhyme came into my head:

Mistress Mary, quite contrary,
How does your garden grow?
With cockle-shells, and silver bells,
And pretty maids all in a row.

97

'Only they are not *cockle* shells, are they, madame? They are *oyster* shells.' His hand pointed.

He heard her catch her breath and then stay very still. Her eyes asked a question.

He nodded. '*Mais, oui*, I know! The maid left the dinner ready – she will swear and Katrina will swear that that is all you had. Only you and your husband know that you brought back a dozen and a half oysters – a little treat *pour la bonne tante*. So easy to put the strychnine in an oyster. It is swallowed – *comme ça*! But there remain the shells – they must not go in the bucket. The maid would see them. And so you thought of making an edging of them to a bed. But there were not enough – the edging is not complete. The effect is bad – it spoils the symmetry of the otherwise charming garden. Those few oyster shells struck an alien note – they displeased my eye on my first visit.'

Mary Delafontaine said, 'I suppose you guessed from the letter. I knew she had written – but I didn't know how much she'd said.'

Poirot answered evasively, 'I knew at least that it was a family matter. If it had been a question of Katrina there would have been no point in hushing things up. I understand that you or your husband handled Miss Barrowby's securities to your own profit, and that she found out –'

Mary Delafontaine nodded. 'We've done it for years – a little here and there. I never realized she was sharp enough to find out. And then I learned she had sent for a detective; and I found out, too, that she was leaving her money to Katrina – that miserable little creature!'

'And so the strychnine was put in Katrina's bedroom? I comprehend. You save yourself and your husband from what I may discover, and you saddle an innocent child with murder. Had you no pity, madame?'

Mary Delafontaine shrugged her shoulders – her blue

forget-me-not eyes looked into Poirot's. He remembered the perfection of her acting the first day he had come and the bungling attempts of her husband. A woman above the average – but inhuman.

She said, 'Pity? For that miserable intriguing little rat?' Her contempt rang out.

Hercule Poirot said slowly, 'I think, madame, that you have cared in your life for two things only. One is your husband.'

He saw her lips tremble.

'And the other – is your garden.'

He looked round him. His glance seemed to apologize to the flowers for that which he had done and was about to do.

The Dead Harlequin

Mr Satterthwaite walked slowly up Bond Street enjoying the sunshine. He was, as usual, carefully and beautifully dressed, and was bound for the Harchester Galleries where there was an exhibition of the paintings of one Frank Bristow, a new and hitherto unknown artist who showed signs of suddenly becoming the rage. Mr Satterthwaite was a patron of the arts.

As Mr Satterthwaite entered the Harchester Galleries, he was greeted at once with a smile of pleased recognition.

'Good morning, Mr Satterthwaite, I thought we should see you before long. You know Bristow's work? Fine – very fine indeed. Quite unique of its kind.'

Mr Satterthwaite purchased a catalogue and stepped through the open archway into the long room where the artist's works were displayed. They were water colours, executed with such extraordinary technique and finish that they resembled coloured etchings. Mr Satterthwaite walked slowly round the walls scrutinizing and, on the whole, approving. He thought that this young man deserved to arrive. Here was originality, vision, and a most severe and exacting technique. There were crudities, of course. That was only to be expected – but there was also something closely allied to genius. Mr Satterthwaite paused before a little masterpiece representing Westminster Bridge with its crowd of buses, trams and hurrying pedestrians. A tiny thing and wonderfully perfect. It was called, he noted, The Ant Heap. He passed on and quite suddenly drew in his breath with a gasp, his imagination held and riveted.

The picture was called The Dead Harlequin. The forefront of it represented a floor of inlaid squares of black and white marble. In the middle of the floor lay Harlequin on his back with his arms outstretched, in his motley of black and red. Behind him was a window and outside that window, gazing in at the figure on the floor, was what appeared to be the same man silhouetted against the red glow of the setting sun.

The picture excited Mr Satterthwaite for two reasons, the first was that he recognized, or thought that he recognized, the face of the man in the picture. It bore a distinct resemblance to a certain Mr Quin, an acquaintance whom Mr Satterthwaite had encountered once or twice under somewhat mystifying circumstances.

'Surely I can't be mistaken,' he murmured. 'If it *is* so – what does it mean?'

For it had been Mr Satterthwaite's experience that every appearance of Mr Quin had some distinct significance attaching to it.

There was, as already mentioned, a second reason for Mr Satterthwaite's interest. He recognized the scene of the picture.

'The Terrace Room at Charnley,' said Mr Satterthwaite. 'Curious – and very interesting.'

He looked with more attention at the picture, wondering what exactly had been in the artist's mind. One Harlequin dead on the floor, another Harlequin looking through the window – or was it the same Harlequin? He moved slowly along the walls gazing at other pictures with unseeing eyes, with his mind always busy on the same subject. He was excited. Life, which had seemed a little drab this morning, was drab no longer. He knew quite certainly that he was on the threshold of exciting and interesting events. He crossed to the table where sat Mr Cobb, a dignitary of the Harchester Galleries, whom he had known for many years.

'I have a fancy for buying no. 39,' he said, 'if it is not already sold.'

Mr Cobb consulted a ledger.

'The pick of the bunch,' he murmured, 'quite a little gem, isn't it? No, it is not sold.' He quoted a price. 'It is a good investment, Mr Satterthwaite. You will have to pay three times as much for it this time next year.'

'That is always said on these occasions,' said Mr Satterthwaite, smiling.

'Well, and haven't I been right?' demanded Mr Cobb. 'I don't believe if you were to sell your collection, Mr Satterthwaite, that a single picture would fetch less than you gave for it.'

'I will buy this picture,' said Mr Satterthwaite. 'I will give you a cheque now.'

'You won't regret it. We believe in Bristow.'

'He is a young man?'

'Twenty-seven or -eight, I should say.'

'I should like to meet him,' said Mr Satterthwaite. 'Perhaps he will come and dine with me one night?'

'I can give you his address. I am sure he would leap at the chance. Your name stands for a good deal in the artistic world.'

'You flatter me,' said Mr Satterthwaite, and was going on when Mr Cobb interrupted:

'Here he is now. I will introduce you to him right away.'

He rose from behind his table. Mr Satterthwaite accompanied him to where a big, clumsy young man was leaning against the wall surveying the world at large from behind the barricade of a ferocious scowl.

Mr Cobb made the necessary introductions and Mr Satterthwaite made a formal and gracious little speech.

'I have just had the pleasure of acquiring one of your pictures – The Dead Harlequin.'

'Oh! Well, you won't lose by it,' said Mr Bristow ungraciously. 'It's a bit of damned good work, although I say it.'

'I can see that,' said Mr Satterthwaite. 'Your work interests me very much, Mr Bristow. It is extraordinarily mature for so young a man. I wonder if you would give me the pleasure of dining with me one night? Are you engaged this evening?'

'As a matter of fact, I am not,' said Mr Bristow, still with no overdone appearance of graciousness.

'Then shall we say eight o'clock?' said Mr Satterthwaite. 'Here is my card with the address on it.'

'Oh, all right,' said Mr Bristow. 'Thanks,' he added as a somewhat obvious afterthought.

'A young man who has a poor opinion of himself and is afraid that the world should share it.'

Such was Mr Satterthwaite's summing up as he stepped out into the sunshine of Bond Street, and Mr Satterthwaite's judgment of his fellow men was seldom far astray.

Frank Bristow arrived about five minutes past eight to find his host and a third guest awaiting him. The other guest was introduced as a Colonel Monckton. They went in to dinner almost immediately. There was a fourth place laid at the oval mahogany table and Mr Satterthwaite uttered a word of explanation.

'I half expected my friend, Mr Quin, might drop in,' he said. 'I wonder if you have ever met him. Mr Harley Quin?'

'I never meet people,' growled Bristow.

Colonel Monckton stared at the artist with the detached interest he might have accorded to a new species of jelly fish. Mr Satterthwaite exerted himself to keep the ball of conversation rolling amicably.

'I took a special interest in that picture of yours because I thought I recognized the scene of it as being the Terrace Room at Charnley. Was I right?' As the artist nodded, he went on. 'That is very interesting. I have stayed at Charnley several times myself in the past. Perhaps you know some of the family?'

'No, I don't!' said Bristow. 'That sort of family wouldn't care to know me. I went there in a charabanc.'

'Dear me,' said Colonel Monckton for the sake of saying something. 'In a charabanc! Dear me.'

Frank Bristow scowled at him.

'Why not?' he demanded ferociously.

Poor Colonel Monckton was taken aback. He looked reproachfully at Mr Satterthwaite as though to say:

'These primitive forms of life may be interesting to you as a naturalist, but why drag *me* in?'

'Oh, beastly things, charabancs!' he said. 'They jolt you so going over the bumps.'

'If you can't afford a Rolls Royce you have got to go in charabancs,' said Bristow fiercely.

Colonel Monckton stared at him. Mr Satterthwaite thought:

'Unless I can manage to put this young man at his ease we are going to have a very distressing evening.'

'Charnley aways fascinated me,' he said. 'I have been there only once since the tragedy. A grim house – and a ghostly one.'

'That's true,' said Bristow.

'There are actually two authentic ghosts,' said Monckton. 'They say that Charles I walks up and down the terrace with his head under his arm – I have forgotten why, I'm sure. Then there is the Weeping Lady with the Silver Ewer, who is always seen after one of the Charnleys dies.'

'Tosh,' said Bristow scornfully.

'They have certainly been a very ill-fated family,' said Mr Satterthwaite hurriedly. 'Four holders of the title have died a violent death and the late Lord Charnley committed suicide.'

'A ghastly business,' said Monckton gravely. 'I was there when it happened.'

'Let me see, that must be fourteen years ago,' said Mr Satterthwaite, 'the house has been shut up ever since.'

'I don't wonder at that,' said Monckton. 'It must have been a terrible shock for a young girl. They had been married a month, just home from their honeymoon. Big fancy dress ball to celebrate their home-coming. Just as the guests were starting to arrive Charnley locked himself into the Oak Parlour and shot himself. That sort of thing isn't done. I beg your pardon?'

He turned his head sharply to the left and looked across at Mr Satterthwaite with an apologetic laugh.

'I am beginning to get the jimjams, Satterthwaite. I thought for a moment there was someone sitting in that empty chair and that he said something to me.

'Yes,' he went on after a minute or two, 'it was a pretty ghastly shock to Alix Charnley. She was one of the prettiest girls you could see anywhere and cram full of what people call the joy of living, and now they say she is like a ghost herself. Not that I have seen her for years. I believe she lives abroad most of the time.'

'And the boy?'

'The boy is at Eton. What he will do when he comes of age I don't know. I don't think, somehow, that he will reopen the old place.'

'It would make a good People's Pleasure Park,' said Bristow.

Colonel Monckton looked at him with cold abhorrence.

'No, no, you don't really mean that,' said Mr Satterthwaite. 'You wouldn't have painted that picture if you did. Tradition and atmosphere are intangible things. They take centuries to build up and if you destroyed them you couldn't rebuild them again in twenty-four hours.'

He rose. 'Let us go into the smoking-room. I have some

photographs there of Charnley which I should like to show you.'

One of Mr Satterthwaite's hobbies was amateur photography. He was also the proud author of a book, 'Homes of My Friends'. The friends in question were all rather exalted and the book itself showed Mr Satterthwaite forth in rather a more snobbish light than was really fair to him.

'That is a photograph I took of the Terrace Room last year,' he said. He handed it to Bristow. 'You see it is taken at almost the same angle as is shown in your picture. That is rather a wonderful rug – it is a pity that photographs can't show colouring.'

'I remember it,' said Bristow, 'a marvellous bit of colour. It glowed like a flame. All the same it looked a bit incongruous there. The wrong size for that big room with its black and white squares. There is no rug anywhere else in the room. It spoils the whole effect – it was like a gigantic blood stain.'

'Perhaps that gave you your idea for your picture?' said Mr Satterthwaite.

'Perhaps it did,' said Bristow thoughtfully. 'On the face of it, one would naturally stage a tragedy in the little panelled room leading out of it.'

'The Oak Parlour,' said Monckton. 'Yes, that is the haunted room right enough. There is a Priests' hiding hole there – a movable panel by the fireplace. Tradition has it that Charles I was concealed there once. There were two deaths from duelling in that room. And it was there, as I say, that Reggie Charnley shot himself.'

He took the photograph from Bristow's hand.

'Why, that is the Bokhara rug,' he said, 'worth a couple of thousand pounds, I believe. When I was there it was in the Oak Parlour – the right place for it. It looks silly on that great expanse of marble flags.'

Mr Satterthwaite was looking at the empty chair which he

had drawn up beside his. Then he said thoughtfully: 'I wonder when it was moved?'

'It must have been recently. Why, I remember having a conversation about it on the very day of the tragedy. Charnley was saying it really ought to be kept under glass.'

Mr Satterthwaite shook his head. 'The house was shut up immediately after the tragedy and everything was left exactly as it was.'

Bristow broke in with a question. He had laid aside his aggressive manner.

'Why did Lord Charnley shoot himself?' he asked.

Colonel Monckton shifted uncomfortably in his chair.

'No one ever knew,' he said vaguely.

'I suppose,' said Mr Satterthwaite slowly, 'that it *was* suicide.'

The Colonel looked at him in blank astonishment.

'Suicide,' he said, 'why, of course it was suicide. My dear fellow, I was there in the house myself.'

Mr Satterthwaite looked towards the empty chair at his side and, smiling to himself as though at some hidden joke the others could not see, he said quietly:

'Sometimes one sees things more clearly years afterwards than one could possibly at the time.'

'Nonsense,' spluttered Monckton, 'arrant nonsense! How can you possibly see things better when they are vague in your memory instead of clear and sharp?'

But Mr Satterthwaite was reinforced from an unexpected quarter.

'I know what you mean,' said the artist. 'I should say that possibly you were right. It is a question of proportion, isn't it? And more than proportion probably. Relativity and all that sort of thing.'

'If you ask me,' said the Colonel, 'all this Einstein business is a lot of dashed nonsense. So are spiritualists and the spook of one's grandmother!' He glared round fiercely.

'Of course it was suicide,' he went on. 'Didn't I practically see the thing happen with my own eyes?'

'Tell us about it,' said Mr Satterthwaite, 'so that we shall see it with our eyes also.'

With a somewhat mollified grunt the Colonel settled himself more comfortably in his chair.

'The whole thing was extraordinarily unexpected,' he began. 'Charnley had been his usual normal self. There was a big party staying in the house for this ball. No one could ever have guessed he would go and shoot himself just as the guests began arriving.'

'It would have been better taste if he had waited until they had gone,' said Mr Satterthwaite.

'Of course it would. Damned bad taste – to do a thing like that.'

'Uncharacteristic,' said Mr Satterthwaite.

'Yes,' admitted Monckton, 'it wasn't like Charnley.'

'And yet it *was* suicide?'

'Of course it was suicide. Why, there were three or four of us there at the top of the stairs. Myself, the Ostrander girl, Algie Darcy – oh, and one or two others. Charnley passed along the hall below and went into the Oak Parlour. The Ostrander girl said there was a ghastly look on his face and his eyes were staring – but, of course, that is nonsense – she couldn't even see his face from where we were – but he did walk in a hunched way, as if he had the weight of the world on his shoulders. One of the girls called to him – she was somebody's governess, I think, whom Lady Charnley had included in the party out of kindness. She was looking for him with a message. She called out "Lord Charnley, Lady Charnley wants to know –" He paid no attention and went into the Oak Parlour and slammed the door and we heard the key turn in the lock. Then, one minute after, *we heard the shot.*

'We rushed down to the hall. There is another door from the Oak Parlour leading into the Terrace Room. We tried that but it was locked, too. In the end we had to break the door down. Charnley was lying on the floor – dead – with a pistol close beside his right hand. Now, what could that have been but suicide? Accident? Don't tell me. There is only one other possibility – murder – and you can't have murder without a murderer. You admit that, I suppose.'

'The murderer might have escaped,' suggested Mr Satterthwaite.

'That is impossible. If you have a bit of paper and a pencil I will draw you a plan of the place. There are two doors into the Oak Parlour, one into the hall and one into the Terrace Room. Both these doors were locked in the inside *and the keys were in the locks.*'

'The window?'

'Shut, and the shutters fastened across it.'

There was a pause.

'So that is that,' said Colonel Monckton triumphantly.

'It certainly seems to be,' said Mr Satterthwaite sadly.

'Mind you,' said the Colonel, 'although I was laughing just now at the spiritualists, I don't mind admitting that there was a deuced rummy atmosphere about the place – about that room in particular. There are several bullet holes in the panels of the walls, the results of the duels that took place in that room, and there is a queer stain on the floor, that always comes back though they have replaced the wood several times. I suppose there will be another blood stain on the floor now – poor Charnley's blood.'

'Was there much blood?' asked Mr Satterthwaite.

'Very little – curiously little – so the doctor said.'

'Where did he shoot himself, through the head?'

'No, through the heart.'

'That is not the easy way to do it,' said Bristow. 'Frightfully

109

difficult to know where one's heart is. I should never do it that way myself.'

Mr Satterthwaite shook his head. He was vaguely dissatisfied. He had hoped to get at something – he hardly knew what. Colonel Monckton went on.

'It is a spooky place, Charnley. Of course, *I* didn't see anything.'

'You didn't see the Weeping Lady with the Silver Ewer?'

'No, I did not, sir,' said the Colonel emphatically. 'But I expect every servant in the place swore they did.'

'Superstition was the curse of the Middle Ages,' said Bristow. 'There are still traces of it here and there, but thank goodness, we are getting free from it.'

'Superstition,' mused Mr Satterthwaite, his eyes turned again to the empty chair. 'Sometimes, don't you think – it might be useful?'

'Bristow stared at him.

'Useful, that's a queer word.'

'Well, I hope you are convinced now, Satterthwaite,' said the Colonel.

'Oh, quite,' said Mr Satterthwaite. 'On the face of it, it seems odd – so purposeless for a newly-married man, young, rich, happy, celebrating his home-coming – curious – but I agree there is no getting away from the facts.' He repeated softly, 'The facts,' and frowned.

'I suppose the interesting thing is a thing we none of us will ever know,' said Monckton, 'the story behind it all. Of course there were rumours – all sorts of rumours. You know the kind of things people say.'

'But no one *knew* anything,' said Mr Satterthwaite thoughtfully.

'It's not a best seller mystery, is it?' remarked Bristow. 'No one gained by the man's death.'

'No one except an unborn child,' said Mr Satterthwaite.

Monckton gave a sharp chuckle. 'Rather a blow to poor Hugo Charnley,' he observed. 'As soon as it was known that there was going to be a child he had the graceful task of sitting tight and waiting to see if it would be a girl or boy. Rather an anxious wait for his creditors, too. In the end a boy it was and a disappointment for the lot of them.'

'Was the widow very disconsolate?' asked Bristow.

'Poor child,' said Monckton, 'I shall never forget her. She didn't cry or break down or anything. She was like something – frozen. As I say, she shut up the house shortly afterwards and, as far as I know, it has never been reopened since.'

'So we are left in the dark as to motive,' said Bristow with a slight laugh. 'Another man or another woman, it must have been one or the other, eh?'

'It seems like it,' said Mr Satterthwaite.

'And the betting is strongly on another woman,' continued Bristow, 'since the fair widow has not married again. I hate women,' he added dispassionately.

Mr Satterthwaite smiled a little and Frank Bristow saw the smile and pounced upon it.

'You may smile,' he said, 'but I do. They upset everything. They interfere. They get between you and your work. They – I only once met a woman who was – well, interesting.'

'I thought there would be one,' said Mr Satterthwaite.

'Not in the way you mean. I – I just met her casually. As a matter of fact – it was in a train. After all,' he added defiantly, 'why shouldn't one meet people in trains?'

'Certainly, certainly,' said Mr Satterthwaite soothingly, 'a train is as good a place as anywhere else.'

'It was coming down from the North. We had the carriage to ourselves. I don't know why, but we began to talk. I don't know her name and I don't suppose I shall ever meet her again. I don't know that I want to. It might be – a pity.' He paused, struggling to express himself. 'She wasn't quite real, you know. Shadowy. Like one of the people who come out of the hills in Gaelic fairy tales.'

Mr Satterthwaite nodded gently. His imagination pictured the scene easily enough. The very positive and realistic Bristow and a figure that was silvery and ghostly – shadowy, as Bristow had said.

'I suppose if something very terrible had happened, so terrible as to be almost unbearable, one might get like that. One might run away from reality into a half world of one's own and then, of course, after a time, one wouldn't be able to get back.'

'Was that what had happened to her?' asked Mr Satterthwaite curiously.

'I don't know,' said Bristow. 'She didn't tell me anything, I am only guessing. One has to guess if one is going to get anywhere.'

'Yes,' said Mr Satterthwaite slowly. 'One has to guess.'

He looked up as the door opened. He looked up quickly and expectantly but the butler's words disappointed him.

'A lady, sir, has called to see you on very urgent business. Miss Aspasia Glen.'

Mr Satterthwaite rose in some astonishment. He knew the name of Aspasia Glen. Who in London did not? First advertised as the Woman with the Scarf, she had given a series of matinées single-handed that had taken London by storm. With the aid of her scarf she had impersonated rapidly various characters. In turn the scarf had been the coif of a nun, the shawl of a mill-worker, the head-dress of a peasant and a hundred other things, and in each impersonation Aspasia Glen had been totally and utterly different. As an artist, Mr Satterthwaite paid full reverence to her. As it happened, he had never made her acquaintance. A call upon him at this unusual hour intrigued him greatly. With a few words of apology to the others he left the room and crossed the hall to the drawing-room.

Miss Glen was sitting in the very centre of a large settee upholstered in gold brocade. So poised she dominated the room. Mr Satterthwaite perceived at once that she meant to dominate the situation. Curiously enough, his first feeling was one of repulsion. He had been a sincere admirer of Aspasia Glen's art. Her personality, as conveyed to him over the footlights, had been appealing and sympathetic. Her effects there had been wistful and suggestive rather than commanding. But now, face to face with the woman herself, he received a totally different impression. There was something hard – bold – forceful about her. She was tall and dark, possibly about thirty-five years of age. She was undoubtedly very good-looking and she clearly relied upon the fact.

'You must forgive this unconventional call, Mr Satterthwaite,' she said. Her voice was full and rich and seductive.

'I won't say that I have wanted to know you for a long time, but I *am* glad of the excuse. As for coming tonight' – she laughed – 'well, when I want a thing, I simply can't wait. When I want a thing, I simply *must* have it.'

'Any excuse that has brought me such a charming lady guest must be welcomed by me,' said Mr Satterthwaite in an old-fashioned gallant manner.

'How nice you are to me,' said Aspasia Glen.

'My dear lady,' said Mr Satterthwaite, 'may I thank you here and now for the pleasure you have so often given me – in my seat in the stalls.'

She smiled delightfully at him.

'I am coming straight to the point. I was at the Harchester Galleries today. I saw a picture there I simply couldn't live without. I wanted to buy it and I couldn't because you had already bought it. So' – she paused – 'I do want it so,' she went on. 'Dear Mr Satterthwaite, I simply *must* have it. I brought my cheque book.' She looked at him hopefully. 'Everyone tells me you are so frightfully kind. People *are* kind to me, you know. It is very bad for me – but there it is.'

So these were Aspasia Glen's methods. Mr Satterthwaite was inwardly coldly critical of this ultra-femininity and of this spoilt child pose. It ought to appeal to him, he supposed, but it didn't. Aspasia Glen had made a mistake. She had judged him as an elderly dilettante, easily flattered by a pretty woman. But Mr Satterthwaite behind his gallant manner had a shrewd and critical mind. He saw people pretty well as they were, not as they wished to appear to him. He saw before him, not a charming woman pleading for a whim, but a ruthless egoist determined to get her own way for some reason which was obscure to him. And he knew quite certainly that Aspasia Glen was not going to get her own way. He was not going to give up the picture of the Dead Harlequin to her. He sought rapidly in his mind for the best way of circumventing her without overt rudeness.

'I am sure,' he said, 'that everyone gives you your own way as often as they can and is only too delighted to do so.'

'Then you are really going to let me have the picture?'

Mr Satterthwaite shook his head slowly and regretfully.

'I am afraid that is impossible. You see' – he paused – 'I bought that picture for a lady. It is a present.'

'Oh! but surely –'

The telephone on the table rang sharply. With a murmured word of excuse Mr Satterthwaite took up the receiver. A voice spoke to him, a small, cold voice that sounded very far away.

'Can I speak to Mr Satterthwaite, please?'

'It is Mr Satterthwaite speaking.'

'I am Lady Charnley, Alix Charnley. I daresay you don't remember me Mr Satterthwaite, it is a great many years since we met.'

'My dear Alix. Of course, I remember you.'

'There is something I wanted to ask you. I was at the

Harchester Galleries at an exhibition of pictures today, there was one called The Dead Harlequin, perhaps you recognized it – it was the Terrace Room at Charnley. I – I want to have that picture. It was sold to you.' She paused. 'Mr Satterthwaite, for reasons of my own I want that picture. Will you resell it to me?'

Mr Satterthwaite thought to himself: 'Why, this is a miracle.' As he spoke into the receiver he was thankful that Aspasia Glen could only hear one side of the conversation. 'If you will accept my gift, dear lady, it will make me very happy.' He heard a sharp exclamation behind him and hurried on. 'I bought it for you. I did indeed. But listen, my dear Alix, I want to ask you to do me a great favour, if you will.'

'Of course. Mr Satterthwaite, I am so *very* grateful.'

He went on. 'I want you to come round now to my house, at once.'

There was a slight pause and then she answered quietly:

'I will come at once.'

Mr Satterthwaite put down the receiver and turned to Miss Glen.

She said quickly and angrily:

'That was the picture you were talking about?'

'Yes,' said Mr Satterthwaite, 'the lady to whom I am presenting it is coming round to this house in a few minutes.'

Suddenly Aspasia Glen's face broke once more into smiles. 'You will give me a chance of persuading her to turn the picture over to me?'

'I will give you a chance of persuading her.'

Inwardly he was strangely excited. He was in the midst of a drama that was shaping itself to some foredoomed end. He, the looker-on, was playing a star part. He turned to Miss Glen.

'Will you come into the other room with me? I should like you to meet some friends of mine.'

He held the door open for her and, crossing the hall, opened the door of the smoking-room.

'Miss Glen,' he said, 'let me introduce you to an old friend of mine, Colonel Monckton. Mr Bristow, the painter of the picture you admire so much.' Then he started as a third figure rose from the chair which he had left empty beside his own.

'I think you expected me this evening,' said Mr Quin. 'During your absence I introduced myself to your friends. I am so glad I was able to drop in.'

'My dear friend,' said Mr Satterthwaite, 'I – I have been carrying on as well as I am able, but –' He stopped before the slightly sardonic glance of Mr Quin's dark eyes. 'Let me introduce you. Mr Harley Quin, Miss Aspasia Glen.'

Was it fancy – or did she shrink back slightly. A curious expression flitted over her face. Suddenly Bristow broke in boisterously. 'I have got it.'

'Got what?'

'Got hold of what was puzzling me. There is a likeness, there is a distinct likeness.' He was staring curiously at Mr Quin. 'You see it?' – he turned to Mr Satterthwaite – 'don't you see a distinct likeness to the Harlequin of my picture – the man looking in through the window?'

It was no fancy this time. He distinctly heard Miss Glen draw in her breath sharply and even saw that she stepped back one pace.

'I told you that I was expecting someone,' said Mr Satterthwaite. He spoke with an air of triumph. 'I must tell you that my friend, Mr Quin, is a most extraordinary person. He can unravel mysteries. He can make you see things.'

'Are you a medium, sir?' demanded Colonel Monckton, eyeing Mr Quin doubtfully.

The latter smiled and slowly shook his head.

'Mr Satterthwaite exaggerates,' he said quietly. 'Once or twice when I have been with him he has done some extraordinarily good deductive work. Why he puts the credit down to me I can't say. His modesty, I suppose.'

'No, no,' said Mr Satterthwaite excitedly. 'It isn't. You make me see things – things that I ought to have seen all along – that I actually have seen – but without knowing that I saw them.'

'It sounds to me deuced complicated,' said Colonel Monckton.

'Not really,' said Mr Quin. 'The trouble is that we are not content just to see things – we will tack the wrong interpretation on to the things we see.'

Aspasia Glen turned to Frank Bristow.

'I want to know,' she said nervously, 'what put the idea of painting that picture into your head?'

Bristow shrugged his shoulders. 'I don't quite know,' he confessed. 'Something about the place – about Charnley, I mean, took hold of my imagination. The big empty room. The terrace outside, the idea of ghosts and things, I suppose. I have just been hearing the tale of the last Lord Charnley, who shot himself. Supposing you are dead, and your spirit lives on? It must be odd, you know. You might stand outside on the terrace looking in at the window at your own dead body, and you would see everything.'

'What do you mean?' said Aspasia Glen. '*See* everything?'

'Well, you would see what happened. You would see –'

The door opened and the butler announced Lady Charnley.

Mr Satterthwaite went to meet her. He had not seen her for nearly thirteen years. He remembered her as she once was, an eager, glowing girl. And now he saw – a Frozen Lady. Very fair, very pale, with an air of drifting rather than walking, a snowflake driven at random by an icy breeze. Something unreal about her. So cold, so far away.

'It was very good of you to come,' said Mr Satterthwaite.

He led her forward. She made a half gesture of recognition towards Miss Glen and then paused as the other made no response.

'I am so sorry,' she murmured, 'but surely I have met you somewhere, haven't I?'

'Over the footlights, perhaps,' said Mr Satterthwaite. 'This is Miss Aspasia Glen, Lady Charnley.'

'I am very pleased to meet you, Lady Charnley,' said Aspasia Glen.

Her voice had suddenly a slight trans-Atlantic tinge to it. Mr Satterthwaite was reminded of one of her various stage impersonations.

'Colonel Monckton you know,' continued Mr Satterthwaite, 'and this is Mr Bristow.'

He saw a sudden faint tinge of colour in her cheeks.

'Mr Bristow and I have met too,' she said, and smiled a little. 'In a train.'

'And Mr Harley Quin.'

He watched her closely, but this time there was no flicker of recognition. He set a chair for her, and then, seating himself, he cleared his throat and spoke a little nervously. 'I – this is rather an unusual little gathering. It centres round this picture. I – I think that if we liked we could – clear things up.'

'You are not going to hold a *séance*, Satterthwaite?' asked Colonel Monckton. 'You are very odd this evening.'

'No,' said Mr Satterthwaite, 'not exactly a *séance*. But my friend, Mr Quin, believes, and I agree, that one can, by looking back over the past, see things as they were and not as they appeared to be.'

'The past?' said Lady Charnley.

'I am speaking of your husband's suicide, Alix. I know it hurts you –'

'No,' said Alix Charnley, 'it doesn't hurt me. Nothing hurts me now.'

Mr Satterthwaite thought of Frank Bristow's words. '*She was not quite real you know. Shadowy. Like one of the people who come out of hills in Gaelic fairy tales.*'

'Shadowy,' he had called her. That described her exactly. A shadow, a reflection of something else. Where then was the real Alix, and his mind answered quickly: '*In the past*. Divided from us by fourteen years of time.'

'My dear,' he said, 'you frighten me. You are like the Weeping Lady with the Silver Ewer.'

Crash! The coffee cup on the table by Aspasia's elbow fell shattered to the floor. Mr Satterthwaite waved aside her apologies. He thought: 'We are getting nearer, we are getting nearer every minute – but nearer to what?'

'Let us take our minds back to that night fourteen years ago,' he said. 'Lord Charnley killed himself. For what reason? No one knows.'

Lady Charnley stirred slightly in her chair.

'Lady Charnley knows,' said Frank Bristow abruptly.

'Nonsense,' said Colonel Monckton, then stopped, frowning at her curiously.

She was looking across at the artist. It was as though he drew the words out of her. She spoke, nodding her head slowly, and her voice was like a snowflake, cold and soft.

'Yes, you are quite right. I *know*. That is why as long as I live I can never go back to Charnley. That is why when my boy Dick wants me to open the place up and live there again I tell him it can't be done.'

'Will you tell us the reason, Lady Charnley?' said Mr Quin.

She looked at him. Then, as though hypnotised, she spoke as quietly and naturally as a child.

'I will tell you if you like. Nothing seems to matter very much now. I found a letter among his papers and I destroyed it.'

'What letter?' said Mr Quin.

'The letter from the girl – from that poor child. She was the Merriams' nursery governess. He had – he had made love to her – yes, while he was engaged to me just before we were married. And she – she was going to have a child too. She wrote saying so, and that she was going to tell me about it. So, you see, he shot himself.'

She looked round at them wearily and dreamily like a child who has repeated a lesson it knows too well.

Colonel Monckton blew his nose.

'My God,' he said, 'so that was it. Well, that explains things with a vengeance.'

'Does it?' said Mr Satterthwaite, 'it doesn't explain one thing. *It doesn't explain why Mr Bristow painted that picture.*'

'What do you mean?'

Mr Satterthwaite looked across at Mr Quin as though for encouragement, and apparently got it, for he proceeded:

'Yes, I know I sound mad to all of you, but that picture is the focus of the whole thing. We are all here tonight because of that picture. That picture *had* to be painted – that is what I mean.'

'You mean the uncanny influence of the Oak Parlour?' began Colonel Monckton.

'No,' said Mr Satterthwaite. '*Not* the Oak Parlour. The Terrace Room. That is it! The spirit of the dead man standing outside the window and looking in and seeing his own dead body on the floor.'

'Which he couldn't have done,' said the Colonel, 'because the body was in the Oak Parlour.'

'Supposing it wasn't,' said Mr Satterthwaite, 'supposing it was exactly where Mr Bristow saw it, saw it imaginatively, I mean on the black and white flags in front of the window.'

'You are talking nonsense,' said Colonel Monckton, 'if it was there we shouldn't have found it in the Oak Parlour.'

'Not unless someone carried it there,' said Mr Satterthwaite.

'And in that case how could we have seen Charnley going in at the door of the Oak Parlour?' inquired Colonel Monckton.

'Well, you didn't see his face, did you?' asked Mr

Satterthwaite. 'What I mean is, you saw a man going into the Oak Parlour in fancy dress, I suppose.'

'Brocade things and a wig,' said Monckton.

'Just so, and you thought it was Lord Charnley because the girl called out to him as Lord Charnley.'

'And because when we broke in a few minutes later there was only Lord Charnley there dead. You can't get away from that, Satterthwaite.'

'No,' said Mr Satterthwaite, discouraged. 'No – unless there was a hiding-place of some kind.'

'Weren't you saying something about there being a Priests' hole in that room?' put in Frank Bristow.

'Oh!' cried Mr Satterthwaite. 'Supposing –?' He waved a hand for silence and sheltered his forehead with his other hand and then spoke slowly and hesitatingly.

'I have got an idea – it may be just an idea, but I think it hangs together. Supposing someone shot Lord Charnley. Shot him in the Terrace Room. Then he – and another person – dragged the body into the Oak Parlour. They laid it down there with the pistol by its right hand. Now we go on to the next step. It must seem absolutely certain that Lord Charnley has committed suicide. I think that could be done very easily. The man in his brocade and wig passes along the hall by the Oak Parlour door and someone, to make sure of things, calls out to him as Lord Charnley from the top of the stairs. He goes in and locks both doors and fires a shot into the wood-work. There were bullet holes already in that room if you remember, one more wouldn't be noticed. He then hides quietly in the secret chamber. The doors are broken open and people rush in. It seems certain that Lord Charnley has committed suicide. No other hypothesis is even entertained.'

'Well, I think that is balderdash,' said Colonel Monckton. 'You forget that Charnley had a motive right enough for suicide.'

'A letter found afterwards,' said Mr Satterthwaite. 'A lying cruel letter written by a very clever and unscrupulous little actress who meant one day to be Lady Charnley herself.'

'You mean?'

'I mean the girl in league with Hugo Charnley,' said Mr Satterthwaite. 'You know, Monckton, everyone knows, that that man was a blackguard. He thought that he was certain to come into the title.' He turned sharply to Lady Charnley. 'What was the name of the girl who wrote that letter?'

'Monica Ford,' said Lady Charnley.

'Was it Monica Ford, Monckton, who called out to Lord Charnley from the top of the stairs?'

'Yes, now you come to speak of it, I believe it was.'

'Oh, that's impossible,' said Lady Charnley. 'I – I went to her about it. She told me it was all true. I only saw her once afterwards, but surely she couldn't have been acting the whole time.'

Mr Satterthwaite looked across the room at Aspasia Glen.

'I think she could,' he said quietly. 'I think she had in her the makings of a very accomplished actress.'

'There is one thing you haven't got over,' said Frank Bristow, 'there would be blood on the floor of the Terrace Room. Bound to be. They couldn't clear that up in a hurry.'

'No,' admitted Mr Satterthwaite, 'but there is one thing they could do – a thing that would only take a second or two – they could throw over the blood-stains the Bokhara rug. Nobody ever saw the Bokhara rug in the Terrace Room before that night.'

'I believe you are right,' said Monckton, 'but all the same those blood-stains would have to be cleared up some time?'

'Yes,' said Mr Satterthwaite, 'in the middle of the night. A woman with a jug and basin could go down the stairs and clear up the blood-stains quite easily.'

'But supposing someone saw her?'

'It wouldn't matter,' said Mr Satterthwaite. 'I am speaking now of things as they *are*. I said a woman with a jug and basin. But if I had said a Weeping Lady with a Silver Ewer that is what they would have *appeared* to be.' He got up and went across to Aspasia Glen. 'That is what you did, wasn't it?' he said. 'They call you the "Woman with the Scarf" now, but it was that night you played your first part, the "Weeping Lady with the Silver Ewer". That is why you knocked the coffee cup off that table just now. You were afraid when you saw that picture. You thought someone knew.'

Lady Charnley stretched out a white accusing hand.

'Monica Ford,' she breathed. 'I recognize you now.'

Aspasia Glen sprang to her feet with a cry. She pushed little Mr Satterthwaite aside with a shove of the hand and stood shaking in front of Mr Quin.

'So I was right. Someone *did* know! Oh, I haven't been deceived by this tomfoolery. This pretence of working things out.' She pointed at Mr Quin. '*You* were there. *You* were there outside the window looking in. You saw what we did, Hugo and I. I *knew* there was someone looking in, I felt it all the time. And yet when I looked up, there was nobody there. I knew someone was watching us. I thought once I caught a glimpse of a face at the window. It has frightened me all these years. Why did you break silence now? That is what I want to know?'

'Perhaps so that the dead may rest in peace,' said Mr Quin.

Suddenly Aspasia Glen made a rush for the door and stood there flinging a few defiant words over her shoulder.

'Do what you like. God knows there are witnesses enough to what I have been saying. I don't care, I don't care. I loved Hugo and I helped him with the ghastly business and he chucked me afterwards. He died last year. You can set the police on my tracks if you like, but as that little dried-up fellow there said, I am a pretty good actress. They will find it hard to find me.' She crashed the door behind her, and a moment later they heard the slam of the front door, also.

'Reggie,' cried Lady Charnley, 'Reggie.' The tears were streaming down her face. 'Oh, my dear, my dear, I can go back to Charnley now. I can live there with Dickie. I can tell him what his father was, the finest, the most splendid man in all the world.'

'We must consult very seriously as to what must be done in the matter,' said Colonel Monckton. 'Alix, my dear, if you will let me take you home I shall be glad to have a few words with you on the subject.'

Lady Charnley rose. She came across to Mr Satterthwaite, and laying both hands on his shoulders, she kissed him very gently.

'It is so wonderful to be alive again after being so long dead,' she said. 'It was like being dead, you know. Thank you, dear Mr Satterthwaite.' She went out of the room with Colonel Monckton. Mr Satterthwaite gazed after them. A grunt from Frank Bristow whom he had forgotten made him turn sharply round.

'She is a lovely creature,' said Bristow moodily. 'But she's not nearly so interesting as she was,' he said gloomily.

'There speaks the artist,' said Mr Satterthwaite.

'Well, she isn't,' said Mr Bristow. 'I suppose I should only get the cold shoulder if I ever went butting in at Charnley. I don't want to go where I am not wanted.'

'My dear young man,' said Mr Satterthwaite, 'if you will think a little less of the impression you are making on other people, you will, I think, be wiser and happier. You would also do well to disabuse your mind of some very old-fashioned notions, one of which is that birth has any significance at all in our modern conditions. You are one of those large proportioned young men whom women always consider good-looking, and you have possibly, if not certainly, genius. Just say that over to yourself ten times before you go to bed every night and in three months' time go and call on Lady Charnley at Charnley. That is my advice to you, and I am an old man with considerable experience of the world.'

A very charming smile suddenly spread over the artist's face.

'You have been thunderingly good to me,' he said suddenly. He seized Mr Sattherthwaite's hand and wrung it in a powerful grip. 'I am no end grateful. I must be off now. Thanks very much for one of the most extraordinary evenings I have ever spent.'

He looked round as though to say goodbye to someone else and then started.

'I say, sir, your friend has gone. I never saw him go. He is rather a queer bird, isn't he?'

'He goes and comes very suddenly,' said Mr Satterthwaite. 'That is one of his characteristics. One doesn't always see him come and go.'

'Like Harlequin,' said Frank Bristow, 'he is invisible,' and laughed heartily at his own joke.

The Gate of Baghdad

I

'Four great gates has the city of Damascus . . .'

Mr Parker Pyne repeated Flecker's lines softly to himself.

*'Postern of Fate, the Desert Gate, Disaster's Cavern, Fort of
Fear,
The Portal of Baghdad am I, the Doorway of Diarbekir.'*

He was standing in the streets of Damascus and drawn up
outside the Oriental Hotel he saw one of the huge six-wheeled
Pullmans that was to transport him and eleven other people
across the desert to Baghdad on the morrow.

*'Pass not beneath, O Caravan, or pass not singing. Have you
heard
That silence where the birds are dead yet something pipeth like
a bird?
Pass out beneath, O Caravan, Doom's Caravan, Death's
Caravan!'*

Something of a contrast now. Formerly the Gate of
Baghdad *had* been the gate of Death. Four hundred miles of
desert to traverse by caravan. Long weary months of travel.
Now the ubiquitous petrol-fed monsters did the journey in
thirty-six hours.

'What were you saying, Mr Parker Pyne?'

It was the eager voice of Miss Netta Pryce, youngest and most charming of the tourist race. Though encumbered by a stern aunt with the suspicion of a beard and a thirst for Biblical knowledge, Netta managed to enjoy herself in many frivolous ways of which the elder Miss Pryce might possibly have not approved.

Mr Parker Pyne repeated Flecker's lines to her.

'How thrilling,' said Netta.

Three men in Air Force uniform were standing near and one of them, an admirer of Netta's, struck in.

'There are still thrills to be got out of the journey,' he said. 'Even nowadays the convoy is occasionally shot up by bandits. Then there's losing yourself – that happens sometimes. And we are sent out to find you. One fellow was lost for five days in the desert. Luckily he had plenty of water with him. Then there are the bumps. Some bumps! One man was killed. It's the truth I'm telling you! He was asleep and his head struck the top of the car and it killed him.'

'In the six-wheeler, Mr O'Rourke?' demanded the elder Miss Pryce.

'No – not in the six-wheeler,' admitted the young man.

'But we must do some sight-seeing,' cried Netta.

Her aunt drew out a guide book.

Netta edged away.

'I know she'll want me to go to some place where St Paul was lowered out of a window,' she whispered. 'And I do so want to see the bazaars.'

O'Rourke responded promptly.

'Come with me. We'll start down the Street called Straight –'

They drifted off.

Mr Parker Pyne turned to a quiet man standing beside him, Hensley by name. He belonged to the public works department of Baghdad.

'Damascus is a little disappointing when one sees it for the first time,' he said apologetically. 'A little civilized. Trams and modern houses and shops.'

Hensley nodded. He was a man of few words.

'Not got – back of beyond – when you think you have,' he jerked out.

Another man drifted up, a fair young man wearing an old Etonian tie. He had an amiable but slightly vacant face which at the moment looked worried. He and Hensley were in the same department.

'Hello, Smethurst,' said his friend. 'Lost anything?'

Captain Smethurst shook his head. He was a young man of somewhat slow intellect.

'Just looking round,' he said vaguely. Then he seemed to rouse himself. 'Ought to have a beano tonight. What?'

The two friends went off together. Mr Parker Pyne bought a local paper printed in French.

He did not find it very interesting. The local news meant nothing to him and nothing of importance seemed to be going on elsewhere. He found a few paragraphs headed *Londres*.

The first referred to financial matters. The second dealt with the supposed destination of Mr Samuel Long, the defaulting financier. His defalcations now amounted to the sum of three millions and it was rumoured that he had reached South America.

'Not too bad for a man just turned thirty,' said Mr Parker Pyne to himself.

'I beg your pardon?'

Parker Pyne turned to confront an Italian General who had been on the same boat with him from Brindisi to Beirut.

Mr Parker Pyne explained his remark. The Italian General nodded his head several times.

'He is a great criminal, that man. Even in Italy we have

128

suffered. He inspired confidence all over the world. He is a man of breeding, too, they say.'

'Well, he went to Eton and Oxford,' said Mr Parker Pyne cautiously.

'Will he be caught, do you think?'

'Depends on how much of a start he got. He may be still in England. He may be – anywhere.'

'Here with us?' the General laughed.

'Possibly.' Mr Parker Pyne remained serious. 'For all you know, General, *I* may be he.'

The General gave him a startled glance. Then his olive-brown face relaxed into a smile of comprehension.

'Oh! That is very good – very good indeed. But you –'

His eyes strayed downwards from Mr Parker Pyne's face. Mr Parker Pyne interpreted the glance correctly.

'You mustn't judge by appearances,' he said. 'A little additional – er – *embonpoint* – is easily managed and has a remarkably ageing effect.'

He added dreamily:

'Then there is hair dye, of course, and face stain, and even a change of nationality.'

General Poli withdrew doubtfully. He never knew how far the English were serious.

Mr Parker Pyne amused himself that evening by going to a cinema. Afterwards he was directed to a 'Nightly Palace of Gaieties'. It appeared to him to be neither a palace nor gay. Various ladies danced with a distinct lack of *verve*. The applause was languid.

Suddenly Mr Parker Pyne caught sight of Smethurst. The young man was sitting at a table alone. His face was flushed and it occurred to Mr Parker Pyne that he had already drunk more than was good for him. He went across and joined the young man.

'Disgraceful, the way these girls treat you,' said Captain

Smethurst gloomily. 'Bought her two drinks – three drinks – lots of drinks. Then she goes off laughing with some dago. Call it a disgrace.'

Mr Parker Pyne sympathized. He suggested coffee.

'Got some *araq* coming,' said Smethurst. 'Jolly good stuff. You try it.'

Mr Parker Pyne knew something of the properties of araq. He employed tact. Smethurst, however, shook his head.

'I'm in a bit of a mess,' he said. 'Got to cheer myself up. Don't know what you'd do in my place. Don't like to go back on a pal, what? I mean to say – and yet – what's a fellow to do?'

He studied Mr Parker Pyne as though noticing him for the first time.

'Who are you?' he demanded with the curtness born of his potations. 'What do you do?'

'The confidence trick,' said Mr Parker Pyne gently.

Smethurst gazed at him in lively concern.

'What – you too?'

Mr Parker Pyne drew from his wallet a cutting. He laid it on the table in front of Smethurst.

'*Are you unhappy?* (So it ran.) *If so, consult Mr Parker Pyne.*'

Smethurst focused on it after some difficulty.

'Well, I'm damned,' he ejaculated. 'You meantersay – people come and tell you things?'

'They confide in me – yes.'

'Pack of idiotic women, I suppose.'

'A good many women,' admitted Mr Parker Pyne. 'But men also. What about you, my young friend? You wanted advice just now?'

'Shut your damned head,' said Captain Smethurst. 'No business of anybody's – anybody's 'cept mine. Where's that goddamed *araq*?'

Mr Parker Pyne shook his head sadly.

He gave up Captain Smethurst as a bad job.

II

The convoy for Baghdad started at seven o'clock in the morning. There was a party of twelve. Mr Parker Pyne and General Poli, Miss Pryce and her niece, three Air Force officers, Smethurst and Hensley and an Armenian mother and son by name Pentemian.

The journey started uneventfully. The fruit trees of Damascus were soon left behind. The sky was cloudy and the young driver looked at it doubtfully once or twice. He exchanged remarks with Hensley.

'Been raining a good bit the other side of Rutbah. Hope we shan't stick.'

They made a halt at midday and square cardboard boxes of lunch were handed round. The two drivers brewed tea which was served in cardboard cups. They drove on again across the flat interminable plain.

Mr Parker Pyne thought of the slow caravans and the weeks of journeying . . .

Just at sunset they came to the desert fort of Rutbah.

The great gates were unbarred and the six-wheeler drove in through them into the inner courtyard of the fort.

'This feels exciting,' said Netta.

After a wash she was eager for a short walk. Flight-Lieutenant O'Rourke and Mr Parker Pyne offered themselves as escorts. As they started the manager came up to them and begged them not to go far away as it might be difficult to find their way back after dark.

'We'll only go a short way,' O'Rourke promised.

Walking was not, indeed, very interesting owing to the sameness of the surroundings.

Once Mr Parker Pyne bent and picked something up.

'What is it?' asked Netta curiously.

He held it out to her.

'A prehistoric flint, Miss Pryce – a borer.'

'Did they – kill each other with them?'

'No – it had a more peaceful use. But I expect they could have killed with it if they'd wanted to. It's the *wish* to kill that counts – the mere instrument doesn't matter. *Something* can always be found.'

It was getting dark, and they ran back to the fort.

After a dinner of many courses of the tinned variety they sat and smoked. At twelve o'clock the six-wheeler was to proceed.

The driver looked anxious.

'Some bad patches near here,' he said. 'We may stick.' They all climbed into the big car and settled themselves. Miss Pryce was annoyed not to be able to get at one of her suitcases.

'I should like my bedroom slippers,' she said.

'More likely to need your gum boots,' said Smethurst. 'If I know the look of things we'll be stuck in a sea of mud.'

'I haven't even got a change of stockings,' said Netta.

'That's all right. You'll stay put. Only the stronger sex has to get out and heave.'

'Always carry spare socks,' said Hensley, patting his overcoat pocket. 'Never know.'

The lights were turned out. The big car started out into the night.

The going was not too good. They were not jolted as they would have been in a touring car, but nevertheless they got a bad bump now and then.

Mr Parker Pyne had one of the front seats. Across the aisle was the Armenian lady shrouded in wraps and shawls. Her son was behind her. Behind Mr Parker Pyne were the two Miss Pryces. The General, Smethurst, Hensley and the R.A.F. men were at the back.

The car rushed on through the night. Mr Parker Pyne found it hard to sleep. His position was cramped. The Armenian lady's feet stuck out and encroached on his preserve. She, at any rate, was comfortable.

Everyone else seemed to be asleep. Mr Parker Pyne felt drowsiness stealing over him, when a sudden jolt threw him towards the roof of the car. He heard a drowsy protest from the back of the six-wheeler. 'Steady. Want to break our necks?'

Then the drowsiness returned. A few minutes later, his neck sagging uncomfortably, Mr Parker Pyne slept . . .

He was awakened suddenly. The six-wheeler had stopped. Some of the men were getting out. Hensley spoke briefly.

'We're stuck.'

Anxious to see all there was to see, Mr Parker Pyne stepped gingerly out in the mud. It was not raining now. Indeed there was a moon and by its light the drivers could be seen frantically at work with jacks and stones, striving to raise the wheels. Most of the men were helping. From the windows of the six-wheeler the three women looked out. Miss Pryce and Netta with interest, the Armenian lady with ill-concealed disgust.

At a command from the driver, the male passengers obediently heaved.

'Where's that Armenian fellow?' demanded O'Rourke. 'Keeping his toes warmed and comfortable like a cat? Let's have him out too.'

'Captain Smethurst too,' observed General Poli. 'He is not with us.'

'The blighter's asleep still. Look at him.'

True enough, Smethurst still sat in his armchair, his head sagging forward and his whole body slumped down.

'I'll rouse him,' said O'Rourke.

He sprang in through the door. A minute later he reappeared. His voice had changed.

'I say. I think he's ill – or something. Where's the doctor?'

Squadron Leader Loftus, the Air Force doctor, a quiet-looking man with greying hair, detached himself from the group at the wheel.

'What's the matter with him?' he asked.

'I – don't know.'

The doctor entered the car. O'Rourke and Parker Pyne followed him. He bent over the sagging figure. One look and touch was enough.

'He's dead,' he said quietly.

'Dead? But how?' Questions shot out. 'Oh! How dreadful!' from Netta.

Loftus turned round in an irritated manner.

'Must have hit his head against the top,' he said. 'We went over one bad bump.'

'Surely that wouldn't kill him? Isn't there anything else?'

'I can't tell you unless I examine him properly,' snapped Loftus. He looked around him with a harassed air. The women were pressing closer. The men outside were beginning to crowd in.

Mr Parker Pyne spoke to the driver. He was a strong athletic young man. He lifted each female passenger in turn, carrying her across the mud and setting her down on dry land. Madame Pentemian and Netta he managed easily, but he staggered under the weight of the hefty Miss Pryce.

The interior of the six-wheeler was left clear for the doctor to make his examination.

The men went back to their efforts to jack up the car. Presently the sun rose over the horizon. It was a glorious day. The mud was drying rapidly, but the car was still stuck. Three jacks had been broken and so far no efforts had been of any avail. The driver started preparing breakfast – opening tins of sausages and boiling tea.

A little way apart Squadron Leader Loftus was giving his verdict.

'There's no mark or wound on him. As I said, he must have hit his head against the top.'

'You're satisfied he died naturally?' asked Mr Parker Pyne.

There was something in his voice that made the doctor look at him quickly.

'There's only one other possibility.'

'Yes.'

'Well, that someone hit him on the back of the head with something in the nature of a sandbag.' His voice sounded apologetic.

'That's not very likely,' said Williamson, the other Air Force officer. He was a cherubic-looking youth. 'I mean, nobody could do that without our seeing.'

'If we were asleep,' suggested the doctor.

'Fellow couldn't be sure of that,' pointed out the other.

'Getting up and all that would have roused someone or other.'

'The only way,' said General Poli, 'would be for anyone sitting behind him. He could choose his moment and need not even rise from his seat.'

'Who was sitting behind Captain Smethurst?' asked the doctor.

O'Rourke replied readily.

'Hensley, sir – so that's no good. Hensley was Smethurst's best pal.'

There was a silence. Then Mr Parker Pyne's voice rose with quiet certainty.

'I think,' he said, 'that Flight Lieutenant Williamson has something to tell us.'

'I, sir? I – well –'

'Out with it, Williamson,' said O'Rourke.

'It's nothing, really – nothing at all.'

'Out with it.'

'It's only a scrap of conversation I overheard – at Rutbah –

in the courtyard. I'd got back into the six-wheeler to look for my cigarette case. I was hunting about. Two fellows were just outside talking. One of them was Smethurst. He was saying –'

He paused.

'Come on, man, out with it.'

'Something about not wanting to let a pal down. He sounded very distressed. Then he said: "I'll hold my tongue till Baghdad – but not a minute afterwards. You'll have to get out quickly".'

'And the other man?'

'I don't know sir. I swear I don't. It was dark and he only said a word or two and that I couldn't catch.'

'Who amongst you knows Smethurst well?'

'I don't think the words – a pal – could refer to anyone but Hensley,' said O'Rourke slowly. 'I knew Smethurst, but very slightly. Williamson is new out – so is Squadron Leader Loftus. I don't think either of them have ever met him before.'

Both men agreed.

'You, General?'

'I never saw the young man until we crossed the Lebanon in the same car from Beirut.'

'And that Armenian rat?'

'He couldn't be a pal,' said O'Rourke with decision. 'And no Armenian would have the nerve to kill anyone.'

'I have, perhaps, a small additional piece of evidence,' said Mr Parker Pyne.

He repeated the conversation he had had with Smethurst in the café at Damascus.

'He made use of the phrase – "don't like to go back on a pal," said O'Rourke thoughtfully. 'And he was worried.'

'Has no one else anything to add?' asked Mr Parker Pyne.

The doctor coughed.

'It may have nothing to do with –' he began.

He was encouraged.

'It was just that I heard Smethurst say to Hensley, "You can't deny that there is a leakage in your department".'

'When was this?'

'Just before starting from Damascus yesterday morning. I thought they were just talking shop. I didn't imagine –' He stopped.

'My friends, this is interesting,' said the General. 'Piece by piece you assemble the evidence.'

'You said a sandbag, doctor,' said Mr Parker Pyne. 'Could a man manufacture such a weapon?'

'Plenty of sand,' said the doctor drily. He took some up in his hand as he spoke.

'If you put some in a sock,' began O'Rourke and hesitated.

Everyone remembered the two short sentences spoken by Hensley the night before.

'*Always carry spare socks. Never know.*'

There was a silence. Then Mr Parker Pyne said quietly, 'Squadron Leader Loftus. I believe Mr Hensley's spare socks are in the pocket of his overcoat which is now in the car.'

Their eyes went for one minute to where a moody figure was pacing to and fro on the horizon. Hensley had held aloof since the discovery of the dead man. His wish for solitude had been respected since it was known that he and the dead man had been friends.

'Will you get them and bring them here?'

The doctor hesitated.

'I don't like –' he muttered. He looked again at that pacing figure. 'Seems a bit low down –'

'You must get them, please,' said Mr Parker Pyne. 'The circumstances are unusual. We are marooned here. And we have got to know the truth. If you will fetch those socks I fancy we shall be a step nearer.'

Loftus turned away obediently.

Mr Parker Pyne drew General Poli a little aside.

'General, I think it was you who sat across the aisle from Captain Smethurst.'

'That is so.'

'Did anyone get up and pass down the car?'

'Only the English lady, Miss Pryce. She went to the wash place at the back.'

'Did she stumble at all?'

'She lurched with the movement of the car, naturally.'

'She was the only person you saw moving about?'

'Yes.'

The General looked at him curiously and said, 'Who are you, I wonder? You take command, yet you are not a soldier.'

'I have seen a good deal of life,' said Mr Parker Pyne.

'You have travelled, eh?'

'No,' said Mr Parker Pyne. 'I have sat in an office.'

Loftus returned carrying the socks. Mr Parker Pyne took them from him and examined them. *To the inside of one of them wet sand still adhered.*

Mr Parker Pyne drew a deep breath.

'Now I know,' he said.

All their eyes went to the pacing figure on the horizon.

'I should like to look at the body if I may,' said Mr Parker Pyne.

He went with the doctor to where Smethurst's body had been laid down covered with a tarpaulin.

The doctor removed the cover.

'There's nothing to see,' he said.

But Mr Parker Pyne's eyes were fixed on the dead man's tie.

'So Smethurst was an old Etonian,' he said.

Loftus looked surprised.

Then Mr Parker Pyne surprised him still further.

'What do you know of young Williamson?' he asked.

'Nothing at all. I only met him at Beirut. I'd come from Egypt. But why? Surely –?'

'Well, it's on his evidence we're going to hang a man, isn't it?' said Mr Parker Pyne cheerfully. 'One's got to be careful.'

He still seemed to be interested in the dead man's tie and collar. He unfastened the studs and removed the collar. Then he uttered an exclamation.

'See that?'

On the back of the collar was a small round bloodstain.

He peered closer down at the uncovered neck.

'This man wasn't killed by a blow on the head, doctor,' he said briskly. 'He was stabbed – at the base of the skull. You can just see the tiny puncture.'

'And I missed it!'

'You'd got your preconceived notion,' said Mr Parker Pyne apologetically. 'A blow on the head. It's easy enough to miss this. You can hardly see the wound. A quick stab with a small sharp instrument and death would be instantaneous. The victim wouldn't even cry out.'

'Do you mean a stiletto? You think the General –?'

'Italians and stilettos go together in the popular fancy – Hallo, here comes a car!'

A touring car appeared over the horizon.

'Good,' said O'Rourke as he came up to join them. 'The ladies can go on in that.'

'What about our murderer?' asked Mr Parker Pyne.

'You mean Hensley –?'

'No, I don't mean Hensley,' said Mr Parker Pyne. 'I happen to know that Hensley's innocent.'

'You – but why?'

'Well, you see, he had sand in his sock.'

O'Rourke stared.

'I know my boy,' said Mr Parker Pyne gently, 'it doesn't sound like sense, but it is. Smethurst wasn't hit on the head, you see, he was stabbed.'

He paused a minute and then went on.

'Just cast your mind back to the conversation I told you about – the conversation we had in the café. You picked out what was, to you, the significant phrase. But it was another phrase that struck me. When I said to him that I did the Confidence Trick he said, "*What, you too?*" Doesn't that strike you as rather curious? I don't know that you'd describe a series of peculations from a Department as a "Confidence Trick". Confidence Trick is more descriptive of someone like the absconding Mr Samuel Long, for instance.'

The doctor started. O'Rourke said: 'Yes – perhaps . . .'

'I said in jest that perhaps the absconding Mr Long was one of our party. Suppose that this is the truth.'

'What – but it's impossible!'

'Not at all. What do you know of people besides their passports and the accounts they give of themselves. Am I really Mr Parker Pyne? Is General Poli really an Italian General? And what of the masculine Miss Pryce senior who needs a shave most distinctly.'

'But he – but Smethurst – didn't know Long?'

'Smethurst is an old Etonian. Long also, was at Eton. Smethurst may have known him although he didn't tell you so. He may have recognized him amongst us. And if so, what is he to do? He has a simple mind, and he worries over the matter. He decides at last to say nothing until Baghdad is reached. But after that he will hold his tongue no longer.'

'You think one of *us* is Long,' said O'Rourke, still dazed.

He drew a deep breath.

'It must be the Italian fellow – it *must* . . . or what about the Armenian?'

'To make up as a foreigner and to get a foreign passport is really much more difficult than to remain English,' said Mr Parker Pyne.

'Miss Pryce?' said O'Rourke incredulously.

'No,' said Mr Parker Pyne. '*This* is our man!'

He laid what seemed an almost friendly hand on the shoulder of the man beside him. But there was nothing friendly in his voice, and the fingers were vice-like in their grip.

'Squadron Leader Loftus or Mr Samuel Long, it doesn't matter what you call him!'

'But that's impossible – impossible,' spluttered O'Rourke. 'Loftus has been in the service for years.'

'But you've never met him before, have you? He was a stranger to all of you. It isn't the *real* Loftus naturally.'

The quiet man found his voice.

'Clever of you to guess. How did you, by the way?'

'Your ridiculous statement that Smethurst had been killed by bumping his head. O'Rourke put that idea into your head when we were standing talking in Damascus yesterday. You thought – how simple! You were the only doctor with us – whatever you said would be accepted. You'd got Loftus's kit. You'd got his instruments. It was easy to select a neat little tool for your purpose. You lean over to speak to him and as you are speaking you drive the little weapon home. You talk a minute or two longer. It is dark in the car. Who will suspect?

'Then comes the discovery of the body. You give your verdict. But it does not go as easily as you thought. Doubts are raised. You fall back on a second line of defence. Williamson repeats the conversation he has overheard Smethurst having with you. It is taken to refer to Hensley and you add a damaging little invention of your own about a leakage in Hensley's department. And then I make a final test. I mention the sand and the socks. You are holding a handful of sand. I send you to find the socks so *that we may know the truth*. But by that I did not mean what you thought I meant. *I had already examined Hensley's socks*. There was no sand in either of them. You put it there.'

Mr Samuel Long lit a cigarette. 'I give it up,' he said. 'My luck's turned. Well, I had a good run while it lasted. They were getting hot on my trail when I reached Egypt. I came across Loftus. He was going to join up in Baghdad – and he knew none of them there. It was too good a chance to be missed. I bought him. It cost me twenty thousand pounds. What was that to me? Then, by cursed ill luck, I run into Smethurst – an ass if there ever was one! He was my fag at Eton. He had a bit of hero worship for me in those days. He didn't like the idea of giving me away. I did my best and at last he promised to say nothing till we reached Baghdad. What chance should I have then? None at all. There was only one way – to eliminate him. But I can assure you I am not a murderer by nature. My talents lie in quite another direction.'

His face changed – contracted. He swayed and pitched forward.

O'Rourke bent over him.

'Probably prussic acid – in the cigarette,' said Mr Parker Pyne. 'The gambler has lost his last throw.'

He looked around him – at the wide desert. The sun beat down on him. Only yesterday they had left Damascus – by the Gate of Baghdad.

'Pass not beneath, O Caravan, or pass not singing. Have you heard
That silence where the birds are dead yet something pipeth like a bird?'

The Case of the Discontented Soldier

I

Major Wilbraham hesitated outside the door of Mr Parker Pyne's office to read, not for the first time, the advertisement from the morning paper which had brought him there. It was simple enough:

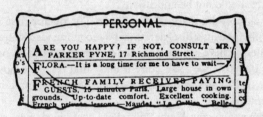

PERSONAL

ARE YOU HAPPY? IF NOT, CONSULT MR. PARKER PYNE, 17 Richmond Street.

FLORA.—It is a long time for me to have to wait—

FRENCH FAMILY RECEIVES PAYING GUESTS, 15 minutes Paris. Large house in own grounds. Up-to-date comfort. Excellent cooking. French private lessons.—Maudet "La Colline," Belle.

The major took a deep breath and abruptly plunged through the swing door leading to the outer office. A plain young woman looked up from her typewriter and glanced at him inquiringly.

'Mr Parker Pyne?' said Major Wilbraham, blushing.

'Come this way, please.'

He followed her into an inner office – into the presence of the bland Mr Parker Pyne.

'Good-morning,' said Mr Pyne. 'Sit down, won't you? And now tell me what I can do for you.'

'My name is Wilbraham –' began the other.

'Major? Colonel?' said Mr Pyne.

'Major.'

'Ah! And recently returned from abroad? India? East Africa?'

'East Africa.'

'A fine country, I believe. Well, so you are home again – and you don't like it. Is that the trouble?'

'You're absolutely right. Though how you knew –'

Mr Parker Pyne waved an impressive hand. 'It is my business to know. You see, for thirty-five years of my life I have been engaged in the compiling of statistics in a government office. Now I have retired and it has occurred to me to use the experience I have gained in a novel fashion. It is all so simple. Unhappiness can be classified under five main headings – no more I assure you. Once you know the cause of a malady, the remedy should not be impossible.

'I stand in the place of the doctor. The doctor first diagnoses the patient's disorder, then he recommends a course of treatment. There are cases where no treatment can be of any avail. If that is so, I say quite frankly that I can do nothing about it. But if I undertake a case, the cure is practically guaranteed.

'I can assure you, Major Wilbraham, that ninety-six per cent of retired empire builders – as I call them – are unhappy. They exchange an active life, a life full of responsibility, a life of possible danger, for – what? Straitened means, a dismal climate and a general feeling of being a fish out of water.'

'All you've said is true,' said the major. 'It's the boredom I object to. The boredom and the endless tittle-tattle about petty village matters. But what can I do about it? I've got a little money besides my pension. I've a nice cottage near Cobham. I can't afford to hunt or shoot or fish. I'm not married. My neighbours are all pleasant folk, but they've no ideas beyond this island.'

'The long and short of the matter is that you find life tame,' said Mr Parker Pyne.

'Damned tame.'

'You would like excitement, possibly danger?' asked Mr Pyne.

The soldier shrugged. 'There's no such thing in this tinpot country.'

'I beg your pardon,' said Mr Pyne seriously. 'There you are wrong. There is plenty of danger, plenty of excitement, here in London if you know where to go for it. You have seen only the surface of our English life, calm, pleasant. But there is another side. If you wish it, I can show you that other side.'

Major Wilbraham regarded him thoughtfully. There was something reassuring about Mr Pyne. He was large, not to say fat; he had a bald head of noble proportions, strong glasses and little twinkling eyes. And he had an aura – an aura of dependability.

'I should warn you, however,' continued Mr Pyne, 'that there is an element of risk.'

The soldier's eye brightened. 'That's all right,' he said. Then, abruptly: 'And – your fees?'

'My fee,' said Mr Pyne, 'is fifty pounds, payable in advance. If in a month's time you are still in the same state of boredom, I will refund your money.'

Wilbraham considered. 'Fair enough,' he said at last. 'I agree. I'll give you a cheque now.'

The transaction was completed. Mr Parker Pyne pressed a buzzer on his desk.

'It is now one o'clock,' he said. 'I am going to ask you to take a young lady out to lunch.' The door opened. 'Ah, Madeleine, my dear, let me introduce Major Wilbraham, who is going to take you out to lunch.'

Wilbraham blinked slightly, which was hardly to be wondered at. The girl who entered the room was dark, languorous, with wonderful eyes and long black lashes, a perfect complexion and a voluptuous scarlet mouth. Her exquisite clothes set off the swaying grace of her figure. From head to foot she was perfect.

'Er – delighted,' said Major Wilbraham.

'Miss de Sara,' said Mr Parker Pyne.

'How very kind of you,' murmured Madeleine de Sara.

'I have your address here,' announced Mr Parker Pyne. 'Tomorrow morning you will receive my further instructions.'

Major Wilbraham and the lovely Madeleine departed.

It was three o'clock when Madeleine returned.

Mr Parker Pyne looked up. 'Well?' he demanded.

Madeleine shook her head. 'Scared of me,' she said. 'Thinks I'm a vamp.'

'I thought as much,' said Mr Parker Pyne. 'You carried out my instructions?'

'Yes. We discussed the occupants of the other tables freely. The type he likes is fair-haired, blue-eyed, slightly anaemic, not too tall.'

'That should be easy,' said Mr Pyne. 'Get me Schedule B and let me see what we have in stock at present.' He ran his finger down a list, finally stopping at a name. 'Freda Clegg. Yes, I think Freda Clegg will do excellently. I had better see Mrs Oliver about it.'

II

The next day Major Wilbraham received a note, which read:

> *On Monday morning next at eleven o'clock go to Eaglemont, Friars Lane, Hampstead, and ask for Mr Jones. You will represent yourself as coming from the Guava Shipping Company.*

Obediently on the following Monday (which happened to be Bank Holiday), Major Wilbraham set out for Eaglemont,

Friars Lane. He set out, I say, but he never got there. For before he got there, something happened.

All the world and his wife seemed to be on their way to Hampstead. Major Wilbraham got entangled in crowds, suffocated in the tube and found it hard to discover the whereabouts of Friars Lane.

Friars Lane was a cul-de-sac, a neglected road full of ruts, with houses on either side standing back from the road. They were largish houses which had seen better days and had been allowed to fall into disrepair.

Wilbraham walked along peering at the half-erased names on the gate-posts, when suddenly he heard something that made him stiffen to attention. It was a kind of gurgling, half-choked cry.

It came again and this time it was faintly recognizable as the word 'Help!' It came from inside the wall of the house he was passing.

Without a moment's hesitation, Major Wilbraham pushed open the rickety gate and sprinted noiselessly up the weed-covered drive. There in the shrubbery was a girl struggling in the grasp of two enormous thugs. She was putting up a brave fight, twisting and turning and kicking. One thug held his hand over her mouth in spite of her furious efforts to get her head free.

Intent on their struggle with the girl, neither of the men had noticed Wilbraham's approach. The first they knew of it was when a violent punch on the jaw sent the man who was covering the girl's mouth reeling backwards. Taken by surprise, the other man relinquished his hold of the girl and turned. Wilbraham was ready for him. Once again his fist shot out, and the thug reeled backwards and fell. Wilbraham turned on the other man, who was closing in behind him.

But the two men had had enough. The second one rolled

over, sat up; then, rising, he made a dash for the gate. His companion followed suit. Wilbraham started after them, but changed his mind and turned towards the girl, who was leaning against a tree, panting.

'Oh, thank you!' she gasped. 'It was terrible.'

Major Wilbraham saw for the first time who it was he had rescued so opportunely. She was a girl of about twenty-one or two, fair-haired and blue-eyed, pretty in a rather colourless way.

'If you hadn't come!' she gasped.

'There, there,' said Wilbraham soothingly. 'It's all right now. I think, though, that we'd better get away from here. It's possible those fellows might come back.'

A faint smile came to the girl's lips. 'I don't think they will – not after the way you hit them. Oh, it was splendid of you!'

Major Wilbraham blushed under the warmth of her glance of admiration. 'Nothin' at all,' he said indistinctly. 'All in day's work. Lady being annoyed. Look here, if you take my arm, can you walk? It's been a nasty shock, I know.'

'I'm all right now,' said the girl. However, she took the proffered arm. She was still rather shaky. She glanced behind her at the house as they emerged through the gate. 'I can't understand it,' she murmured. 'That's clearly an empty house.'

'It's empty, right enough,' agreed the major, looking up at the shuttered windows and general air of decay.

'And yet it *is* Whitefriars.' She pointed to a half-obliterated name on the gate. 'And Whitefriars was the place I was to go.'

'Don't worry about anything now,' said Wilbraham. 'In a minute or two we'll be able to get a taxi. Then we'll drive somewhere and have a cup of coffee.'

At the end of the lane they came out into a more frequented street, and by good fortune a taxi had just set down a fare at one of the houses. Wilbraham hailed it, gave an address to the driver and they got in.

'Don't try to talk,' he admonished his companion. 'Just lie back. You've had a nasty experience.'

She smiled at him gratefully.

'By the way – er – my name is Wilbraham.'

'Mine is Clegg – Freda Clegg.'

Ten minutes later, Freda was sipping hot coffee and looking gratefully across a small table at her rescuer.

'It seems like a dream,' she said. 'A bad dream.' She shuddered. 'And only a short while ago I was wishing for something to happen – anything! Oh, I don't like adventures.'

'Tell me how it happened.'

'Well, to tell you properly I shall have to talk a lot about myself, I'm afraid.'

'An excellent subject,' said Wilbraham, with a bow.

'I am an orphan. My father – he was a sea captain – died when I was eight. My mother died three years ago. I work in the city. I am with the Vacuum Gas Company – a clerk. One evening last week I found a gentleman waiting to see me when I returned to my lodgings. He was a lawyer, a Mr Reid from Melbourne.

'He was very polite and asked me several questions about my family. He explained that he had known my father many years ago. In fact, he had transacted some legal business for him. Then he told me the object of his visit. "Miss Clegg," he said, "I have reason to suppose that you might benefit as the result of a financial transaction entered into by your father several years before he died." I was very much surprised, of course.

'"It is unlikely that you would ever have heard anything of the matter," he explained. "John Clegg never took the affair seriously, I fancy. However, it has materialized unexpectedly, but I am afraid any claim you might put in would depend on your ownership of certain papers. These papers would be part of your father's estate, and of course it is possible that they have been destroyed as worthless. Have you kept any of your father's papers?"

'I explained that my mother had kept various things of my father's in an old sea chest. I had looked through it cursorily, but had discovered nothing of interest.

'"You would hardly be likely to recognize the importance of these documents, perhaps," he said, smiling.

'Well, I went to the chest, took out the few papers it contained and brought them to him. He looked at them, but said it was impossible to say off-hand what might or might not be connected with the matter in question. He would take them away with him and would communicate with me if anything turned up.

'By the last post on Saturday I received a letter from him in which he suggested that I come to his house to discuss the matter. He gave me the address: Whitefriars, Friars Lane, Hampstead. I was to be there at a quarter to eleven this morning.

'I was a little late finding the place. I hurried through the gate and up towards the house, when suddenly those two dreadful men sprang at me from the bushes. I hadn't time to cry out. One man put his hand over my mouth. I wrenched my head free and screamed for help. Luckily you heard me. If it hadn't been for you –' She stopped. Her looks were more eloquent than further words.

'Very glad I happened to be on the spot. By Gad, I'd like to get hold of those two brutes. You'd never seen them before, I suppose?'

She shook her head. 'What do you think it means?'

'Difficult to say. But one thing seems pretty sure. There's something someone wants among your father's papers. This man Reid told you a cock-and-bull story so as to get the opportunity of looking through them. Evidently what he wanted wasn't there.'

'Oh!' said Freda. 'I wonder. When I got home on Saturday I thought my things had been tampered with. To tell you the truth, I suspected my landlady of having pried about in my room out of curiosity. But now –'

'Depend upon it, that's it. Someone gained admission to your room and searched it, without finding what he was after. He suspected that you knew the value of this paper, whatever it was, and that you carried it about on your person. So he planned this ambush. If you'd had it with you, it would have been taken from you. If not, you would have been held prisoner while he tried to make you tell where it was hidden.'

'But what can it possibly *be*?' cried Freda.

'I don't know. But it must be something pretty good for him to go to this length.'

'It doesn't seem possible.'

'Oh, I don't know. Your father was a sailor. He went to out-of-the-way places. He might have come across something the value of which he never knew.'

'Do you really think so?' A pink flush of excitement showed in the girl's pale cheeks.

'I do indeed. The question is, what shall we do next? You don't want to go to the police, I suppose?'

'Oh, no, please.'

'I'm glad you say that. I don't see what good the police could do, and it would only mean unpleasantness for you. Now I suggest that you allow me to give you lunch somewhere and that I then accompany you back to your lodgings, so as to be sure you reach them safely. And then, we might have a look for the paper. Because, you know, it must be somewhere.'

'Father may have destroyed it himself.'

'He may, of course, but the other side evidently doesn't think so, and that looks hopeful for us.'

'What do you think it can be? Hidden treasure?'

'By jove, it might be!' exclaimed Major Wilbraham, all the

boy in him rising joyfully to the suggestion. 'But now, Miss Clegg, lunch!'

They had a pleasant meal together. Wilbraham told Freda all about his life in East Africa. He described elephant hunts, and the girl was thrilled. When they had finished, he insisted on taking her home in a taxi.

Her lodgings were near Notting Hill Gate. On arriving there, Freda had a brief conversation with her landlady. She returned to Wilbraham and took him up to the second floor, where she had a tiny bedroom and sitting-room.

'It's exactly as we thought,' she said. 'A man came on Saturday morning to see about laying a new electric cable; he told her there was a fault in the wiring in my room. He was there some time.'

'Show me this chest of your father's,' said Wilbraham.

Freda showed him a brass-bound box. 'You see,' she said, raising the lid, 'it's empty.'

The soldier nodded thoughtfully. 'And there are no papers anywhere else?'

'I'm sure there aren't. Mother kept everything in here.'

Wilbraham examined the inside of the chest. Suddenly he uttered an exclamation. 'Here's a slit in the lining.' Carefully he inserted his hand, feeling about. A slight crackle rewarded him. 'Something's slipped down behind.'

In another minute he had drawn out his find. A piece of dirty paper folded several times. He smoothed it out on the table; Freda was looking over his shoulder. She uttered an exclamation of disappointment.

'It's just a lot of queer marks.'

'Why, the thing's in Swahili. *Swahili*, of all things!' cried Major Wilbraham. 'East African native dialect, you know.'

'How extraordinary!' said Freda. 'Can you read it, then?'

'Rather. But what an amazing thing.' He took the paper to the window.

'Is it anything?' asked Freda tremulously. Wilbraham read the thing through twice, and then came back to the girl. 'Well,' he said, with a chuckle, 'here's your hidden treasure, all right.'

'Hidden treasure? Not *really*? You mean Spanish gold – a sunken galleon – that sort of thing?'

'Not quite so romantic as that, perhaps. But it comes to the same thing. This paper gives the hiding-place of a cache of ivory.'

'Ivory?' said the girl, astonished.

'Yes. Elephants, you know. There's a law about the number you're allowed to shoot. Some hunter got away with breaking that law on a grand scale. They were on his trail and he cached the stuff. There's a thundering lot of it – and this gives fairly clear directions how to find it. Look here, we'll have to go after this, you and I.'

'You mean there's really a lot of money in it?'

'Quite a nice little fortune for you.'

'But how did that paper come to be among my father's things?'

Wilbraham shrugged. 'Maybe the Johnny was dying or something. He may have written the thing down in Swahili for protection and given it to your father, who possibly had befriended him in some way. Your father, not being able to read it, attached no importance to it. That's only a guess on my part, but I dare say it's not far wrong.'

Freda gave a sigh. 'How frightfully exciting!'

'The thing is – what to do with the precious document,' said Wilbraham. 'I don't like leaving it here. They might come and have another look. I suppose you wouldn't entrust it to me?'

'Of course I would. But – mightn't it be dangerous for you?' she faltered.

'I'm a tough nut,' said Wilbraham grimly. 'You needn't worry about me.' He folded up the paper and put it in his pocket-book. 'May I come to see you tomorrow evening?' he asked. 'I'll have worked out a plan by then, and I'll look up the places on my map. What time do you get back from the city?'

'I get back about half-past six.'

'Capital. We'll have a powwow and then perhaps you'll let me take you out to dinner. We ought to celebrate. So long, then. Tomorrow at half-past six.'

Major Wilbraham arrived punctually on the following day. He rang the bell and enquired for Miss Clegg. A maid-servant had answered the door.

'Miss Clegg? She's out.'

'Oh!' Wilbraham did not like to suggest that he come in and wait. 'I'll call back presently,' he said.

He hung about in the street opposite, expecting every minute to see Freda tripping towards him. The minutes passed. Quarter to seven. Seven. Quarter-past seven. Still no Freda. A feeling of uneasiness swept over him. He went back to the house and rang the bell again.

'Look here,' he said, 'I had an appointment with Miss Clegg at half-past six. Are you sure she isn't in or hasn't – er – left any message?'

'Are you Major Wilbraham?' asked the servant.

'Yes.'

'Then there's a note for you. It come by hand.'

Dear Major Wilbraham, – Something rather strange has happened. I won't write more now, but will you meet me at Whitefriars? Go there as soon as you get this.
Yours sincerely,
Freda Clegg

Wilbraham drew his brows together as he thought rapidly. His hand drew a letter absent-mindedly from his pocket. It was to his tailor. 'I wonder,' he said to the maid-servant, 'if you could let me have a stamp.'

'I expect Mrs Parkins could oblige you.'

She returned in a moment with the stamp. It was paid for with a shilling. In another minute Wilbraham was walking towards the tube station, dropping the envelope in a box as he passed.

Freda's letter had made him most uneasy. What could have taken the girl, alone, to the scene of yesterday's sinister encounter?

He shook his head. Of all the foolish things to do! Had Reid appeared? Had he somehow or other prevailed upon the girl to trust him? What had taken her to Hampstead?

He looked at his watch. Nearly half-past seven. She would have counted on his starting at half-past six. An hour late. Too much. If only she had had the sense to give him some hint.

The letter puzzled him. Somehow its independent tone was not characteristic of Freda Clegg.

It was ten minutes to eight when he reached Friars Lane. It was getting dark. He looked sharply about him; there was no one in sight. Gently he pushed the rickety gate so that it swung noiselessly on its hinges. The drive was deserted. The house was dark. He went up the path cautiously, keeping a look out from side to side. He did not intend to be caught by surprise.

Suddenly he stopped. Just for a minute a chink of light had shone through one of the shutters. The house was not empty. There was someone inside.

Softly Wilbraham slipped into the bushes and worked his way round to the back of the house. At last he found what he was looking for. One of the windows on the ground floor was unfastened. It was the window of a kind of scullery. He raised the sash, flashed a torch he had brought around the deserted interior and climbed in.

Carefully he opened the scullery door. There was no sound. He flashed the torch once more. A kitchen – empty. Outside the kitchen were half a dozen steps and a door evidently leading to the front part of the house.

He pushed open the door and listened. Nothing. He slipped through. He was now in the front hall. Still there was no sound. There was a door to the right and a door to the left. He chose the right-hand door, listened for a time, then turned the handle. It gave. Inch by inch he opened the door and stepped inside.

Again he flashed the torch. The room was unfurnished and bare.

Just at that moment he heard a sound behind him, whirled round – too late. Something came down on his head and he pitched forward into unconsciousness . . .

How much time elapsed before he regained consciousness Wilbraham had no idea. He returned painfully to life, his head aching. He tried to move and found it impossible. He was bound with ropes.

His wits came back to him suddenly. He remembered now. He had been hit on the head.

A faint light from a gas jet high up on the wall showed him that he was in a small cellar. He looked around and his heart gave a leap. A few feet away lay Freda, bound like himself. Her eyes were closed, but even as he watched her anxiously, she sighed and they opened. Her bewildered gaze fell on him and joyous recognition leaped into them.

'You, too!' she said. 'What has happened?'

'I've let you down badly,' said Wilbraham. 'Tumbled head-long into the trap. Tell me, did you send me a note asking me to meet you here?'

The girl's eyes opened in astonishment. '*I*? But you sent *me* one.'

'Oh, I sent you one, did I?'

'Yes. I got it at the office. It asked me to meet you here instead of at home.'

'Same method for both of us,' he groaned, and he explained the situation.

'I see,' said Freda. 'Then the idea was –?'

'To get the paper. We must have been followed yesterday. That's how they got on to me.'

'And – have they got it?' asked Freda.

'Unfortunately, I can't feel and see,' said the soldier, regarding his bound hands ruefully.

And then they both started. For a voice spoke, a voice that seemed to come from the empty air.

'Yes, thank you,' it said. 'I've got it, all right. No mistake about that.'

The unseen voice made them both shiver.

'Mr Reid,' murmured Freda.

'Mr Reid is one of my names, my dear young lady,' said the voice. 'But only one of them. I have a great many. Now, I am sorry to say that you two have interfered with my plans – a thing I never allow. Your discovery of this house is a serious matter. You have not told the police about it yet, but you might do so in the future.

'I very much fear that I cannot trust you in the matter. You might promise – but promises are seldom kept. And, you see, this house is very useful to me. It is, you might say, my clearing house. The house from which there is no return. From here you pass on – elsewhere. You, I am sorry to say, are so passing on. Regrettable – but necessary.'

The voice paused for a brief second, then resumed: 'No bloodshed. I abhor bloodshed. My method is much simpler. And really not too painful, so I understand. Well, I must be getting along. Good-evening to you both.'

'Look here!' It was Wilbraham who spoke. 'Do what you like to me, but this young lady has done nothing – nothing. It can't hurt you to let her go.'

But there was no answer.

At that moment there came a cry from Freda. 'The water – the water!'

Wilbraham twisted himself painfully and followed the direction of her eyes. From a hole up near the ceiling a steady trickle of water was pouring in.

Freda gave a hysterical cry. 'They're going to drown us!'

The perspiration broke out on Wilbraham's brow. 'We're not done yet,' he said. 'We'll shout for help. Surely somebody will hear us. Now, both together.'

They yelled and shouted at the tops of their voices. Not until they were hoarse did they stop.

'No use, I'm afraid,' said Wilbraham sadly. 'We're too far underground and I expect the doors are muffled. After all, if we could be heard, I've no doubt that brute would have gagged us.'

'Oh,' cried Freda. 'And it's all my fault. I got you into this.'

'Don't worry about that, little girl. It's you I'm thinking about. I've been in tight corners before now and got out of them. Don't you lose heart. I'll get you out of this. We've plenty of time. At the rate that water's flowing in, it will be hours before the worst happens.'

'How wonderful you are!' said Freda. 'I've never met anybody like you – except in books.'

'Nonsense – just common sense. Now, I've got to loosen these infernal ropes.'

At the end of a quarter of an hour, by dint of straining and twisting, Wilbraham had the satisfaction of feeling that his bonds were appreciably loosened. He managed to bend his head down and his wrists up till he was able to attack the knots with his teeth.

Once his hands were free, the rest was only a matter of time. Cramped, stiff, but free, he bent over the girl. A minute later she was also free.

So far the water was only up to their ankles.

'And now,' said the soldier, 'to get out of here.'

The door of the cellar was up a few stairs. Major Wilbraham examined it.

'No difficulty here,' he said. 'Flimsy stuff. It will soon give at the hinges.' He set his shoulders to it and heaved.

There was a cracking of wood – a crash, and the door burst from its hinges.

Outside was a flight of stairs. At the top was another door – a very different affair – of solid wood, barred with iron.

'A bit more difficult, this,' said Wilbraham. 'Hallo, here's a piece of luck. It's unlocked.'

He pushed it open, peered round it, then beckoned the girl to come on. They emerged into a passage behind the kitchen. In another moment they were standing under the stars in Friars Lane.

'Oh!' Freda gave a little sob. 'Oh, how dreadful it's been!'

'My poor darling.' He caught her in his arms. 'You've been so wonderfully brave. Freda – darling angel – could you ever – I mean, would you – I love you, Freda. Will you marry me?'

After a suitable interval, highly satisfactory to both parties, Major Wilbraham said, with a chuckle:

'And what's more, we've still got the secret of the ivory cache.'

'But they took it from you!'

The major chuckled again. 'That's just what they didn't do! You see, I wrote out a proof copy, and before joining you here tonight, I put the real thing in a letter I was sending to my tailor and posted it. They've got the spoof copy – and I wish them joy of it! Do you know what we'll do, sweetheart! We'll go to East Africa for our honeymoon and hunt out the cache.'

III

Mr Parker Pyne left his office and climbed two flights of stairs. Here in a room at the top of the house sat Mrs Oliver, the sensational novelist, now a member of Mr Pyne's staff.

Mr Parker Pyne tapped at the door and entered. Mrs Oliver sat at a table on which were a typewriter, several notebooks, a general confusion of loose manuscripts and a large bag of apples.

'A very good story, Mrs Oliver,' said Mr Parker Pyne genially.

'It went off well?' said Mrs Oliver. 'I'm glad.'

'That water-in-the-cellar business,' said Mr Parker Pyne. 'You don't think, on a future occasion, that something more original – perhaps?' He made the suggestion with proper diffidence.

Mrs Oliver shook her head and took an apple from her bag. 'I think not, Mr Pyne. You see, people are used to reading about such things. Water rising in a cellar, poison gas, et cetera. Knowing about it beforehand gives it an extra thrill when it happens to oneself. The public is conservative, Mr Pyne; it likes the old well-worn gadgets.'

'Well, you should know,' admitted Mr Parker Pyne, mindful of the authoress's forty-six successful works of fiction, all best sellers in England and America, and freely translated into French, German, Italian, Hungarian, Finnish, Japanese and Abyssinian. 'How about expenses?'

Mrs Oliver drew a paper towards her. 'Very moderate, on the whole. The two thugs, Percy and Jerry, wanted very little. Young Lorrimer, the actor, was willing to enact the part of Mr Reid for five guineas. The cellar speech was a phonograph record, of course.'

'Whitefriars has been extremely useful to me,' said Mr

Pyne. 'I bought it for a song and it has already been the scene of eleven exciting dramas.'

'Oh, I forgot,' said Mrs Oliver. 'Johnny's wages. Five shillings.'

'Johnny?'

'Yes. The boy who poured the water from the watering cans through the hole in the wall.'

'Ah yes. By the way, Mrs Oliver, how did you happen to know Swahili?'

'I didn't.'

'I see. The British Museum perhaps?'

'No. Delfridge's Information Bureau.'

'How marvellous are the resources of modern commerce!' he murmured.

'The only thing that worries me,' said Mrs Oliver, 'is that those two young people won't find any cache when they get there.'

'One cannot have everything in this world,' said Mr Parker Pyne. 'They will have had a honeymoon.'

IV

Mrs Wilbraham was sitting in a deck-chair. Her husband was writing a letter. 'What's the date, Freda?'

'The sixteenth.'

'The sixteenth. By jove!'

'What is it, dear?'

'Nothing. I just remembered a chap named Jones.'

However happily married, there are some things one never tells.

'Dash it all,' thought Major Wilbraham. 'I ought to have called at that place and got my money back.' And then, being a fair-minded man, he looked at the other side of the question. 'After all, it was I who broke the bargain. I suppose if I'd gone to see Jones something would have happened. And, anyway, as it turns out, if I hadn't been going to see Jones, I should never have heard Freda cry for help, and we might never have met. So, indirectly, perhaps they have a right to the fifty pounds!'

Mrs Wilbraham was also following out a train of thought. 'What a silly little fool I was to believe in that advertisement and pay those people three guineas. Of course, they never did anything for it and nothing ever happened. If I'd only known what was coming – first Mr Reid, and then the queer, romantic way that Charlie came into my life. And to think that but for pure chance *I might never have met him!*'

She turned and smiled adoringly at her husband.

The Man in the Mist

Tommy was not pleased with life. Blunt's Brilliant Detectives had met with a reverse, distressing to their pride if not to their pockets. Called in professionally to elucidate the mystery of a stolen pearl necklace at Adlington Hall, Adlington, Blunt's Brilliant Detectives had failed to make good. Whilst Tommy, hard on the track of a gambling Countess, was tracking her in the disguise of a Roman Catholic priest, and Tuppence was 'getting off' with the nephew of the house on the golf links, the local Inspector of Police had unemotionally arrested the second footman who proved to be a thief well known at headquarters, and who admitted his guilt without making any bones about it.

Tommy and Tuppence, therefore, had withdrawn with what dignity they could muster, and were at the present moment solacing themselves with cocktails at the Grand Adlington Hotel. Tommy still wore his clerical disguise.

'Hardly a Father Brown touch, that,' he remarked gloomily. 'And yet I've got just the right kind of umbrella.'

'It wasn't a Father Brown problem,' said Tuppence. 'One needs a certain atmosphere from the start. One must be doing something quite ordinary, and then bizarre things begin to happen. That's the idea.'

'Unfortunately,' said Tommy, 'we have to return to town. Perhaps something bizarre will happen on the way to the station.'

163

He raised the glass he was holding to his lips, but the liquid in it was suddenly spilled, as a heavy hand smacked him on the shoulder, and a voice to match the hand boomed out words of greeting.

'Upon my soul, it is! Old Tommy! And Mrs Tommy too. Where did you blow in from? Haven't seen or heard anything of you for years.'

'Why, it's Bulger!' said Tommy, setting down what was left of the cocktail, and turning to look at the intruder, a big square-shouldered man of thirty years of age, with a round red beaming face, and dressed in golfing kit. 'Good old Bulger!'

'But I say, old chap,' said Bulger (whose real name, by the way, was Marvyn Estcourt), 'I never knew you'd taken orders. Fancy you a blinking parson.'

Tuppence burst out laughing, and Tommy looked embarrassed. And then they suddenly became conscious of a fourth person.

A tall, slender creature, with very golden hair and very round blue eyes, almost impossibly beautiful, with an effect of really expensive black topped by wonderful ermines, and very large pearl earrings. She was smiling. And her smile said many things. It asserted, for instance, that she knew perfectly well that she herself was the thing best worth looking at, certainly in England, and possibly in the whole world. She was not vain about it in any way, but she just knew, with certainty and confidence, that it was so.

Both Tommy and Tuppence recognised her immediately. They had seen her three times in *The Secret of the Heart*, and an equal number of times in that other great success, *Pillars of Fire*, and in innumerable other plays. There was, perhaps, no other actress in England who had so firm a hold on the British public, as Miss Gilda Glen. She was reported to be the most beautiful woman in England. It was also rumoured that she was the stupidest.

'Old friends of mine, Miss Glen,' said Estcourt, with a tinge of apology in his voice for having presumed, even for a moment, to forget such a radiant creature. 'Tommy and Mrs Tommy, let me introduce you to Miss Gilda Glen.'

The ring of pride in his voice was unmistakable. By merely being seen in his company, Miss Glen had conferred great glory upon him.

The actress was staring with frank interest at Tommy.

'Are you really a priest?' she asked. 'A Roman Catholic priest, I mean? Because I thought they didn't have wives.'

Estcourt went off in a boom of laughter again.

'That's good,' he exploded. 'You sly dog, Tommy. Glad he hasn't renounced you, Mrs Tommy, with all the rest of the pomps and vanities.'

Gilda Glen took not the faintest notice of him. She continued to stare at Tommy with puzzled eyes.

'Are you a priest?' she demanded.

'Very few of us are what we seem to be,' said Tommy gently. 'My profession is not unlike that of a priest. I don't give absolution – but I listen to confessions – I –'

'Don't you listen to him,' interrupted Estcourt. 'He's pulling your leg.'

'If you're not a clergyman, I don't see why you're dressed up like one,' she puzzled. 'That is, unless –'

'Not a criminal flying from justice,' said Tommy. 'The other thing.'

'Oh!' she frowned, and looked at him with beautiful bewildered eyes.

'I wonder if she'll ever get that,' thought Tommy to himself. 'Not unless I put it in words of one syllable for her, I should say.'

Aloud he said:

'Know anything about the trains back to town, Bulger? We've got to be pushing for home. How far is it to the station?'

'Ten minutes' walk. But no hurry. Next train up is the 6.35 and it's only about twenty to six now. You've just missed one.'

'Which way is it to the station from here?'

'Sharp to the left when you turn out of the hotel. Then – let me see – down Morgan's Avenue would be the best way, wouldn't it?'

'Morgan's Avenue?' Miss Glen started violently, and stared at him with startled eyes.

'I know what you're thinking of,' said Estcourt, laughing. 'The Ghost. Morgan's Avenue is bounded by the cemetery on one side, and tradition has it that a policeman who met his death by violence gets up and walks on his old beat, up and down Morgan's Avenue. A spook policeman! Can you beat it? But lots of people swear to having seen him.'

'A policeman?' said Miss Glen. She shivered a little. 'But there aren't really any ghosts, are there? I mean – there aren't such things?'

She got up, folding her wrap tighter round her.

'Goodbye,' she said vaguely.

She had ignored Tuppence completely throughout, and now she did not even glance in her direction. But, over her shoulder, she threw one puzzled questioning glance at Tommy.

Just as she got to the door, she encountered a tall man with grey hair and a puffy face, who uttered an exclamation of surprise. His hand on her arm, he led her through the doorway, talking in an animated fashion.

'Beautiful creature, isn't she?' said Estcourt. 'Brains of a rabbit. Rumour has it that she's going to marry Lord Leconbury. That was Leconbury in the doorway.'

'He doesn't look a very nice sort of man to marry,' remarked Tuppence.

Estcourt shrugged his shoulders.

'A title has a kind of glamour still, I suppose,' he said. 'And Leconbury is not an impoverished peer by any means. She'll be in clover. Nobody knows where she sprang from. Pretty near the gutter, I dare say. There's something deuced mysterious about her being down here anyway. She's not staying at the hotel. And when I tried to find out where she was staying, she snubbed me – snubbed me quite crudely, in the only way she knows. Blessed if I know what it's all about.'

He glanced at his watch and uttered an exclamation.

'I must be off. Jolly glad to have seen you two again. We must have a bust in town together some night. So long.'

He hurried away, and as he did so, a page approached with a note on a salver. The note was unaddressed.

'But it's for you, sir,' he said to Tommy. 'From Miss Gilda Glen.'

Tommy tore it open and read it with some curiosity. Inside were a few lines written in a straggling untidy hand.

I'm not sure, but I think you might be able to help me. And you'll be going that way to the station. Could you be at The White House, Morgan's Avenue, at ten minutes past six?
    Yours sincerely,
      Gilda Glen.

Tommy nodded to the page, who departed, and then handed the note to Tuppence.

'Extraordinary!' said Tuppence. 'Is it because she still thinks you're a priest?'

'No,' said Tommy thoughtfully. 'I should say it's because she's at last taken in that I'm not one. Hullo! what's this?'

'This,' was a young man with flaming red hair, a pugnacious jaw, and appallingly shabby clothes. He had walked into the room and was now striding up and down muttering to himself.

'Hell!' said the red-haired man, loudly and forcibly. 'That's what I say – Hell!'

He dropped into a chair near the young couple and stared at them moodily.

'Damn all women, that's what I say,' said the young man, eyeing Tuppence ferociously. 'Oh! all right, kick up a row if you like. Have me turned out of the hotel. It won't be for the first time. Why shouldn't we say what we think? Why should we go about bottling up our feelings, and smirking, and saying things exactly like everyone else. I don't feel pleasant and polite. I feel like getting hold of someone round the throat and gradually choking them to death.'

He paused.

'Any particular person?' asked Tuppence. 'Or just anybody?'

'One particular person,' said the young man grimly.

'This is very interesting,' said Tuppence. 'Won't you tell us some more?'

'My name's Reilly,' said the red-haired man. 'James Reilly. You may have heard it. I wrote a little volume of Pacifist poems – good stuff, although I say so.'

'*Pacifist poems*?' said Tuppence.

'Yes – why not?' demanded Mr Reilly belligerently.

'Oh! nothing,' said Tuppence hastily.

'I'm for peace all the time,' said Mr Reilly fiercely. 'To Hell with war. And women! Women! Did you see that creature who was trailing around here just now? Gilda Glen, she calls herself. Gilda Glen! God! how I've worshipped that woman. And I'll tell you this – if she's got a heart at all, it's on my side. She cared once for me, and I could make her care again. And if she sells herself to that muck heap, Leconbury – well, God help her. I'd as soon kill her with my own hands.'

And on this, suddenly, he rose and rushed from the room.

Tommy raised his eyebrows.

'A somewhat excitable gentleman,' he murmured. 'Well, Tuppence, shall we start?'

A fine mist was coming up as they emerged from the hotel into the cool outer air. Obeying Estcourt's directions, they turned sharp to the left, and in a few minutes they came to a turning labelled Morgan's Avenue.

The mist had increased. It was soft and white, and hurried past them in little eddying drifts. To their left was the high wall of the cemetery, on their right a row of small houses. Presently these ceased, and a high hedge took their place.

'Tommy,' said Tuppence. 'I'm beginning to feel jumpy. The mist – and the silence. As though we were miles from anywhere.'

'One does feel like that,' agreed Tommy. 'All alone in the world. It's the effect of the mist, and not being able to see ahead of one.'

Tuppence nodded.

'Just our footsteps echoing on the pavement. What's that?'

'What's what?'

'I thought I heard other footsteps behind us.'

'You'll be seeing the ghost in a minute if you work yourself up like this,' said Tommy kindly. 'Don't be so nervy. Are you afraid the spook policeman will lay his hands on your shoulder?'

Tuppence emitted a shrill squeal.

'Don't, Tommy. Now you've put it into my head.'

She craned her head back over her shoulder, trying to peer into the white veil that was wrapped all round them.

'There they are again,' she whispered. 'No, they're in front now. Oh! Tommy, don't say you can't hear them?'

'I do hear something. Yes, it's footsteps behind us. Somebody else walking this way to catch the train. I wonder –'

He stopped suddenly, and stood still, and Tuppence gave a gasp.

For the curtain of mist in front of them suddenly parted in the most artificial manner, and there, not twenty feet away, a gigantic policeman suddenly appeared, as though materialised out of the fog. One minute he was not there, the next minute he was – so at least it seemed to the rather superheated imaginations of the two watchers. Then as the mist rolled back still more, a little scene appeared, as though set on a stage.

The big blue policeman, a scarlet pillar box, and on the right of the road the outlines of a white house.

'Red, white, and blue,' said Tommy. 'It's damned pictorial. Come on, Tuppence, there's nothing to be afraid of.'

For, as he had already seen, the policeman was a real policeman. And, moreover, he was not nearly so gigantic as he had at first seemed looming up out of the mist.

But as they started forward, footsteps came from behind them. A man passed them, hurrying along. He turned in at the gate of the white house, ascended the steps, and beat a deafening tattoo upon the knocker. He was admitted just as they reached the spot where the policeman was standing staring after him.

'There's a gentleman seems to be in a hurry,' commented the policeman.

He spoke in a slow reflective voice, as one whose thoughts took some time to mature.

'He's the sort of gentleman always would be in a hurry,' remarked Tommy.

The policeman's stare, slow and rather suspicious, came round to rest on his face.

'Friend of yours?' he demanded, and there was distinct suspicion now in his voice.

'No,' said Tommy. 'He's not a friend of mine, but I happen to know who he is. Name of Reilly.'

'Ah!' said the policeman. 'Well, I'd better be getting along.'

'Can you tell me where the White House is?' asked Tommy.

The constable jerked his head sideways.

'This is it. Mrs Honeycott's.' He paused, and added, evidently with the idea of giving them valuable information,

'Nervous party. Always suspecting burglars is around. Always asking me to have a look around the place. Middle-aged women get like that.'

'Middle-aged, eh?' said Tommy. 'Do you happen to know if there's a young lady staying there?'

'A young lady,' said the policeman, ruminating. 'A young lady. No, I can't say I know anything about that.'

'She mayn't be staying here, Tommy,' said Tuppence. 'And anyway, she mayn't be here yet. She could only have started just before we did.'

'Ah!' said the policeman suddenly. 'Now that I call it to mind, a young lady did go in at this gate. I saw her as I was coming up the road. About three or four minutes ago it might be.'

'With ermine furs on?' asked Tuppence eagerly.

'She had some kind of white rabbit round her throat,' admitted the policeman.

Tuppence smiled. The policeman went on in the direction from which they had just come, and they prepared to enter the gate of the White House.

Suddenly, a faint, muffled cry sounded from inside the house, and almost immediately afterwards the front door opened and James Reilly came rushing down the steps. His face was white and twisted, and his eyes glared in front of him unseeingly. He staggered like a drunken man.

He passed Tommy and Tuppence as though he did not see them, muttering to himself with a kind of dreadful repetition.

'My God! My God! Oh, my God!'

He clutched at the gatepost, as though to steady himself, and then, as though animated by sudden panic, he raced off down the road as hard as he could go in the opposite direction from that taken by the policeman.

II

Tommy and Tuppence stared at each other in bewilderment.

'Well,' said Tommy, 'something's happened in that house to scare our friend Reilly pretty badly.'

Tuppence drew her finger absently across the gatepost.

'He must have put his hand on some wet red paint somewhere,' she said idly.

'H'm,' said Tommy. 'I think we'd better go inside rather quickly. I don't understand this business.'

In the doorway of the house a white-capped maid-servant was standing, almost speechless with indignation.

'Did you ever see the likes of that now, Father,' she burst out, as Tommy ascended the steps. 'That fellow comes here, asks for the young lady, rushes upstairs without how or by your leave. She lets out a screech like a wild cat – and what wonder, poor pretty dear, and straightaway he comes rushing down again, with the white face on him, like one who's seen a ghost. What will be the meaning of it all?'

'Who are you talking with at the front door, Ellen?' demanded a sharp voice from the interior of the hall.

'Here's Missus,' said Ellen, somewhat unnecessarily.

She drew back, and Tommy found himself confronting a grey-haired, middle-aged woman, with frosty blue eyes imperfectly concealed by pince-nez, and a spare figure clad in black with bugle trimming.

'Mrs Honeycott?' said Tommy. 'I came here to see Miss Glen.'

'Mrs Honeycott gave him a sharp glance, then went on to Tuppence and took in every detail of her appearance.

'Oh, you did, did you?' she said. 'Well, you'd better come inside.'

She led the way into the hall and along it into a room at the back of the house, facing on the garden. It was a fair-sized room, but looked smaller than it was, owing to the large amount of chairs and tables crowded into it. A big fire burned in the grate, and a chintz-covered sofa stood at one side of it. The wallpaper was a small grey stripe with a festoon of roses round the top. Quantities of engravings and oil paintings covered the walls.

It was a room almost impossible to associate with the expensive personality of Miss Gilda Glen.

'Sit down,' said Mrs Honeycott. 'To begin with, you'll excuse me if I say I don't hold with the Roman Catholic religion. Never did I think to see a Roman Catholic priest in my house. But if Gilda's gone over to the Scarlet Woman, it's only what's to be expected in a life like hers – and I dare say it might be worse. She mightn't have any religion at all. I should think more of Roman Catholics if their priests were married – I always speak my mind. And to think of those convents – quantities of beautiful young girls shut up there, and no one knowing what becomes of them – well, it won't bear thinking about.'

Mrs Honeycott came to a full stop, and drew a deep breath.

Without entering upon a defence of the celibacy of the priesthood or the other controversial points touched upon, Tommy went straight to the point.

'I understand, Mrs Honeycott, that Miss Glen is in this house.'

'She is. Mind you, I don't approve. Marriage is marriage and your husband's your husband. As you make your bed, so you must lie on it.'

'I don't quite understand –' began Tommy, bewildered.

'I thought as much. That's the reason I brought you in here. You can go up to Gilda after I've spoken my mind. She came to me – after all these years, think of it! – and asked me to help her. Wanted me to see this man and persuade him to agree to a divorce. I told her straight out I'd have nothing whatever to do with it. Divorce is sinful. But I couldn't refuse my own sister shelter in my house, could I now?'

'Your sister?' exclaimed Tommy.

'Yes, Gilda's my sister. Didn't she tell you?'

Tommy stared at her openmouthed. The thing seemed fantastically impossible. Then he remembered that the angelic beauty of Gilda Glen had been in evidence for many years. He had been taken to see her act as quite a small boy. Yes, it was possible after all. But what a piquant contrast. So it was from this lower middle-class respectability that Gilda Glen had sprung. How well she had guarded her secret!

'I am not yet quite clear,' he said. 'Your sister is married?'

'Ran away to be married as a girl of seventeen,' said Mrs Honeycott succinctly. 'Some common fellow far below her in station. And our father a reverend. It was a disgrace. Then she left her husband and went on the stage. Play-acting! I've never been inside a theatre in my life. I hold no truck with wickedness. Now, after all these years, she wants to divorce the man. Means to marry some big wig, I suppose. But her husband's standing firm – not to be bullied and not to be bribed – I admire him for it.'

'What is his name?' asked Tommy suddenly.

'That's an extraordinary thing now, but I can't remember! It's nearly twenty years ago, you know, since I heard it. My father forbade it to be mentioned. And I've refused to discuss the matter with Gilda. She knows what I think, and that's enough for her.'

'It wasn't Reilly, was it?'

'Might have been. I really can't say. It's gone clean out of my head.'

'The man I mean was here just now.'

'That man! I thought he was an escaped lunatic. I'd been in the kitchen giving orders to Ellen. I'd just got back into this room, and was wondering whether Gilda had come in yet (she has a latchkey), when I heard her. She hesitated a minute or two in the hall and then went straight upstairs. About three minutes later all this tremendous rat-tatting began. I went out into the hall, and just saw a man rushing upstairs. Then there was a sort of cry upstairs, and presently down he came again and rushed out like a madman. Pretty goings on.'

Tommy rose.

'Mrs Honeycott, let us go upstairs at once. I am afraid –'

'What of?'

'Afraid that you have no red wet paint in the house.'

Mrs Honeycott stared at him.

'Of course I haven't.'

'That is what I feared,' said Tommy gravely. 'Please let us go to your sister's room at once.'

Momentarily silenced, Mrs Honeycott led the way. They caught a glimpse of Ellen in the hall, backing hastily into one of the rooms.

Mrs Honeycott opened the first door at the top of the stairs. Tommy and Tuppence entered close behind her.

Suddenly she gave a gasp and fell back.

A motionless figure in black and ermine lay stretched on the sofa. The face was untouched, a beautiful soulless face like a mature child asleep. The wound was on the side of the head, a heavy blow with some blunt instrument had crushed in the skull. Blood was dripping slowly on to the floor, but the wound itself had long ceased to bleed . . .

Tommy examined the prostrate figure, his face very white.

'So,' he said at last, 'he didn't strangle her after all.'

'What do you mean? Who?' cried Mrs Honeycott. 'Is she dead?'

'Oh, yes, Mrs Honeycott, she's dead. Murdered. The question is – by whom? Not that it is much of a question. Funny – for all his ranting words, I didn't think the fellow had got it in him.'

He paused a minute, then turned to Tuppence with decision.

'Will you go out and get a policeman, or ring up the police station from somewhere?'

Tuppence nodded. She too, was very white. Tommy led Mrs Honeycott downstairs again.

'I don't want there to be any mistake about this,' he said. 'Do you know exactly what time it was when your sister came in?'

'Yes, I do,' said Mrs Honeycott. 'Because I was just setting the clock on five minutes as I have to do every evening. It loses just five minutes a day. It was exactly eight minutes past six by my watch, and that never loses or gains a second.'

Tommy nodded. That agreed perfectly with the policeman's story. He had seen the woman with the white furs go in at the gate, probably three minutes had elapsed before he and Tuppence had reached the same spot. He had glanced at his own watch then and had noted that it was just one minute after the time of their appointment.

There was just the faint chance that some one might have been waiting for Gilda Glen in the room upstairs. But if so, he must still be hiding in the house. No one but James Reilly had left it.

He ran upstairs and made a quick but efficient search of the premises. But there was no one concealed anywhere.

Then he spoke to Ellen. After breaking the news to her, and waiting for her first lamentations and invocations to the saints to have exhausted themselves, he asked a few questions.

Had any one else come to the house that afternoon asking for Miss Glen? No one whatsoever. Had she herself been upstairs at all that evening? Yes she'd gone up at six o'clock as usual to draw the curtains – or it might have been a few minutes after six. Anyway it was just before that wild fellow came breaking the knocker down. She'd run downstairs to

176

answer the door. And him a black-hearted murderer all the time.

Tommy let it go at that. But he still felt a curious pity for Reilly, and unwillingness to believe the worst of him. And yet there was no one else who could have murdered Gilda Glen. Mrs Honeycott and Ellen had been the only two people in the house.

He heard voices in the hall, and went out to find Tuppence and the policeman from the beat outside. The latter had produced a notebook, and a rather blunt pencil, which he licked surreptitiously. He went upstairs and surveyed the victim stolidly, merely remarking that if he was to touch anything the Inspector would give him beans. He listened to all Mrs Honeycott's hysterical outbursts and confused explanations, and occasionally he wrote something down. His presence was calming and soothing.

Tommy finally got him alone for a minute or two on the steps outside ere he departed to telephone headquarters.

'Look here,' said Tommy, 'you saw the deceased turning in at the gate, you say. Are you sure she was alone?'

'Oh! she was alone all right. Nobody with her.'

'And between that time and when you met us, nobody came out of the gate?'

'Not a soul.'

'You'd have seen them if they had?'

'Of course I should. Nobody come out till that wild chap did.'

The majesty of the law moved portentously down the steps and paused by the white gatepost, which bore the imprint of a hand in red.

'Kind of amateur he must have been,' he said pityingly. 'To leave a thing like that.'

Then he swung out into the road.

III

It was the day after the crime. Tommy and Tuppence were still at the Grand Hotel, but Tommy had thought it prudent to discard his clerical disguise.

James Reilly had been apprehended, and was in custody. His solicitor, Mr Marvell, had just finished a lengthy conversation with Tommy on the subject of the crime.

'I never would have believed it of James Reilly,' he said simply. 'He's always been a man of violent speech, but that's all.'

Tommy nodded.

'If you disperse energy in speech, it doesn't leave you too much over for action. What I realise is that I shall be one of the principal witnesses against him. That conversation he had with me just before the crime was particularly damning. And, in spite of everything, I like the man, and if there was anyone else to suspect, I should believe him to be innocent. What's his own story?'

The solicitor pursed up his lips.

'He declares that he found her lying there dead. But that's impossible, of course. He's using the first lie that comes into his head.'

'Because, if he happened to be speaking the truth, it would mean that the garrulous Mrs Honeycott committed the crime – and that is fantastic. Yes, he must have done it.'

'The maid heard her cry out, remember.'

'The maid – yes –'

Tommy was silent a moment. Then he said thoughtfully.

'What credulous creatures we are, really. We believe evidence as though it were gospel truth. And what is it really? Only the impression conveyed to the mind by the senses – and suppose they're the wrong impressions?'

The lawyer shrugged his shoulders.

'Oh! we all know that there are unreliable witnesses, witnesses who remember more and more as time goes on, with no real intention to deceive.'

'I don't mean only that. I mean all of us – we say things that aren't really so, and never know that we've done so. For instance, both you and I, without doubt, have said some time or other, "There's the post," when what we really meant was that we'd heard a double knock and the rattle of the letter-box. Nine times out of ten we'd be right, and it would be the post, but just possibly the tenth time it might be only a little urchin playing a joke on us. See what I mean?'

'Ye-es,' said Mr Marvell slowly. 'But I don't see what you're driving at?'

'Don't you? I'm not so sure that I do myself. But I'm beginning to see. It's like the stick, Tuppence. You remember? One end of it pointed one way – but the other end always points the opposite way. It depends whether you get hold of it by the right end. Doors open – but they also shut. People go upstairs, but they also go downstairs. Boxes shut, but they also open.'

'What *do* you mean?' demanded Tuppence.

'It's so ridiculously easy, really,' said Tommy. 'And yet it's only just come to me. How do you know when a person's come into the house. You hear the door open and bang to, and if you're expecting any one to come in, you will be quite sure it is them. But it might just as easily be someone going *out.*'

'But Miss Glen didn't go out?'

'No, I know *she* didn't. But some one else did – the murderer.'

'But how did she get in, then?'

'She came in whilst Mrs Honeycott was in the kitchen talking to Ellen. They didn't hear her. Mrs Honeycott went back to the drawing-room, wondered if her sister had come in and began to put the clock right, and then, as she thought, she heard her come in and go upstairs.'

'Well, what about that? The footsteps going upstairs?'

'That was Ellen, going up to draw the curtains. You remember, Mrs Honeycott said her sister paused before going up. That pause was just the time needed for Ellen to come out from the kitchen into the hall. She just missed seeing the murderer.'

'But, Tommy,' cried Tuppence. 'The cry she gave?'

'That was James Reilly. Didn't you notice what a high-pitched voice he has? In moments of great emotion, men often squeal just like a woman.'

'But the murderer? We'd have seen him?'

'We *did* see him. We even stood talking to him. Do you remember the sudden way that policeman appeared? That was because he stepped out of the gate, just after the mist cleared from the road. It made us jump, don't you remember? After all, though we never think of them as that, policemen are men just like any other men. They love and they hate. They marry . . .

'I think Gilda Glen met her husband suddenly just outside that gate, and took him in with her to thrash the matter out. He hadn't Reilly's relief of violent words, remember. He just saw red – and he had his truncheon handy . . .'